FORGOTTEN LIVES

Where Evil Lurks

Book 1

In the

NINTH MIRACLE TRILOGY

FORGOTTEN LIVES: *Where Evil Lurks*

FORGOTTEN LIVES

Where Evil Lurks

SHERRY BRISCOE

CHAT NOIR PRESS

Chat Noir Press, LLC
P.O. Box 663
Eagle, ID 83616

http://ChatNoirPress.wordpress.com

To all the women in my life, my mother, my aunts, my sisters, my daughters, and my friends – You are the soul of the universe.

Table of Contents

FORGOTTEN LIVES: *Where Evil Lurks*

MAYA

The Humanitarian

Gabriella Santos sat in the back seat of her foster parent's car as they pulled into the parking lot of the counseling center. She held her backpack tight in her hands, watching the rain wash over the thick stone walls of the century-old building.

"It's rumored this place is haunted," Gabriella said.

Mr. Pond replied from the driver's seat. "It's not haunted. There's no such thing as ghosts."

Mrs. Pond looked at her husband beside her. "We need to get going if we're going to meet the Lund's on time."

"We'll be back to pick you up in an hour," Mr. Pond said over his shoulder.

Gabriella's dark eyes showed no surprise. She nodded her acceptance and ambled into the four-story building, letting the August rain wash over her.

Gabriella paused at the reception desk to the left of the large lobby. "I need to use the restroom before I check in, if that's okay?"

"Of course," Gloria, the young lady behind the glass said, "I'll let your counselor know you're here."

Gabriella made her way down the hall where she met Maya Sanderson, the center's director.

"Gabriella, you're all wet. We have some towels to dry off with, if you'd like."

"Thank you, Mrs. Sanderson, I'm fine," Gabriella said, clutching her backpack tighter to her chest.

"Well you let your counselor know if you want one, okay?"

Gabriella looked up at Maya. "Thank you, I will." She stopped at the door of the restroom, and looked back at Maya. "Mrs. Sanderson, do you believe in ghosts and demons?"

Maya stopped on her way into the records room. "I do. I believe in ghosts, demons, angels, and all manner of unexplainable things that go bump in the night." Maya's eyes lit up with child-like imagination and she chuckled. It made Gabriella smile back.

Inside the women's restroom, Gabriella stood in the center of the empty room and gazed out the small window high on the outside wall as the rain washed over the textured glass. She placed her worn backpack on the counter. One corner of the bag was held together by safety pins, torn and frayed like her life. Gabriella pulled out a small prescription bottle, and poured the last three capsules into her palm. Tossing them in her mouth as she tilted her head back, she washed them down with a handful of water she cupped in her other hand.

Gabriella threw the prescription bottle in the trash can, and then pulled out a picture of her mother and her when she was four years old. She didn't remember it being taken, but she loved the feeling the photo inspired, to see her and her mother sitting on the steps of a porch soaking up the sunlight, a cool drink in their hands and laughing. She'd forgotten what her mother's laugh sounded like.

She set the picture face down on the counter next to the sink.

Gabriella pulled out a small bottle of perfume, squirted a burst of lilac fragrance on the back of the picture, then onto herself. She took in a deep wavering breath and opened a small envelope dropping its contents onto the sterile bathroom counter.

A shiny razor blade.

Gabriella stared at the razor for a moment, not blinking, and hardly breathing. She looked into the mirror, her eyes welled up with tears and one escaped down her cheek as gently as the droplets of rain fell over the window outside. She made the sign of the cross over her forehead and shoulders as her Catholic upbringing had taught her, and whispered, "Forgive me Father."

Footsteps approached the bathroom. Gabriella snatched the razor blade and ducked into the end stall, latching the door. She waited in silence as her heart pounded. The voices on the other side of the door continued on down the hall and she was left alone.

Holding the razor blade firm in her fingers, Gabriella sat down on the floor and gritted her teeth as she sliced quick and deep across one wrist severing the main artery, winced, then quickly cut the other.

Outside, the rain continued to fall.

Inside, Gabriella fell for the last time. Her blood seeped along the cracks of the old tile floor and one arm extended beyond the boundaries of the stall.

Upstairs on the second floor, Maya sat in her office and chatted with a difficult stake holder on the telephone.

"I understand Mrs. Moore, but these things have to be approached carefully. I do appreciate your concern, and I assure you, we're doing all we can. Yes, thank you, Mrs. Moore." Maya released a sigh of relief as she hung up the phone. "Now back to this grant work." She mumbled to herself, reached for her coffee cup and returned her focus to her computer screen.

The tile floors of the large building echoed the running footsteps that rushed to her door. Maya sat her coffee cup down on its coaster and looked up.

"What's all the commotion? It sounds like a fire drill minus the alarm."

June stood in the doorway bouncing franticly, gesturing down the hall. "Maya, you have to come right away. It's terrible!"

Maya didn't need to ask what it was, her intuition had already guessed, to some degree, tragedy had struck the center. She was right.

Sirens blared on the street as gasps of horror echoed through the hallways. Maya stood inside the restroom that was covered in blood. Her chest was felt constricted with panic.

"Is she dead?" June asked from behind.

Maya spun around. "Get the paramedics in here!" she yelled down the hall.

The center was flooded with police, firemen and paramedics. Maya asked the counselors to send all the clients home. The staff waited in their offices for answers. Two uniformed officers collected information.

Officer Lopez radioed in. "We need a detective at the Treasure Valley Counseling center. Fourteen year old female found dead on site. Affirmative." He turned to Maya. "Detective Hardy will be here shortly to go over a few things with you. Considering her age, and that she's a ward of the state, there are certain procedures that have to be followed." He turned and assisted the other officer in the restroom with the paramedics.

Maya's heart wanted to explode, it was beating so fast. *How could this happen?* She walked over to the reception area. "Please call anyone who has appointments for the rest of today and reschedule. I don't want anyone else coming in here today." She walked back to the mass of emergency personnel and stood vigilant as they carried out their duties.

They cleared out one by one, and Maya stood by as they wheeled Gabriella out to an ambulance. She stepped in the restroom that was now empty, but covered in blood, and shook her head in sorrow. She came out and walked over to the reception area again.

"Please call our housekeeping service, we need them to come in now and clean that room. I don't want to see one drop of blood when they're done," Maya said. She turned around and faced a man in a suit standing behind her. He held his hand out.

"I'm Detective Ray Hardy with the Caldwell Police." He pulled a badge and a business card from his inside pocket and offered them to Maya.

She held the card in her hands, but couldn't read it through blurry eyes. She slid it in her pocket. "What can I do for you?" Maya asked, her voice full of sorrow, her eyes red.

Detective Hardy put the badge back in his inside pocket, revealing his shoulder holster and gun. "Mrs. Sanderson, I'm sorry for this tragedy here at the Children's Home. I'll be investigating Miss Santos' death. Is there someplace we can talk?"

Maya motioned for him to follow her, and they walked upstairs to her corner office. She could not contain her tears, and wiped her eyes. "It's not a children's home anymore, this center hasn't housed children since 1975."

"Yes, I know, I'm sorry. I grew up not far from here when it was an orphanage. I guess I still refer to it that way out of habit." His voice and brown eyes were sincere.

17

They got to her office and Detective Hardy sat down in a comfortable chair across from Maya's desk. She pulled a Kleenex out of its box and wiped her eyes and nose.

"Detective Hardy, I would love to help you, but we can't comment on this and we can't release her records."

Detective Hardy paused and looked down at his hands that rested in his lap. "I understand. I just need to collect a few facts. For instance, who was the last person to see Gabriella?"

Maya's eyes widened. "Me," she said in a soft voice.

"Did she give any indication that she was upset? We need to ascertain first if this was in fact a suicide, or something else."

Maya sat back defiantly. "It was not anything else. There was no one there but her."

"Are you absolutely sure of that?"

Maya nodded yes.

"I will need to talk to her counselor, and will put in a request for her records if needed. I'm also going to talk to her foster parents, and anyone else that can give us some more insight."

Maya sat there in a daze. "I don't understand this at all."

"Did she say anything to you before she entered the restroom?" Detective Hardy asked.

Maya thought for a moment. "She asked me if I believe in ghosts and demons." She turned to look out the window. The rain had turned to a drizzle.

Detective Hardy stood up and slipped his notepad into his inside pocket. "I'll keep you posted, but if nothing unusual comes up, we should have this wrapped up in a week or so. But also, if you can think of anything else, please call me."

Maya turned back around to look at him. She stood up, sucked in a deep breath, and lead the detective to the door. "I'll escort you out."

The clacking of Maya's heels on the tile floors echoed through the wide hallway and down the stairs, through the empty building.

The drizzle stopped, leaving behind puddles of fresh water for children to stomp in. Maya eased back in her leather chair; her heart heavy with pain, her head slowly shook in denial. She had witnessed many things at the center during her tenure, some happy, some sad. But she had not witnessed death until today. Mascara tinged tears ran down her cheeks leaving crooked trails through her make up. Her breath escaped on a heavy sigh.

Maya picked up her cell phone. She typed a text message to her fifteen-year old son, Michael. "Pizza tonight?"

Her phone whistled with its reply, "Pepperoni and a movie?"

Maya's dimples defied a downpour of tears. "It's a date." She texted back. "luv Mom."

Wiping her nose, Maya grabbed her laptop and purse, and headed out the door. In the hallway of the second floor she peeked into June's office.

"June, I'm going home. I'll see you in the morning. Call my cell if you need anything."

June nodded. "Of course, I'm almost out of here too."

Maya hurried down to the first floor and checked in with the ladies in the reception area. "I'm headed out; call me if you need anything," She said, hoping they wouldn't. She turned and continued through the large entry, and down the steps of the stone complex spanning half the city block.

Maya called her fiancé, Jon, from her car.

"Hi babe, what's up?" Jon answered in his Texas drawl.

"Ga…" her words froze in her mouth.

"Babe? What's the matter?"

Maya closed her eyes, tugged at the seat belt strapped across her chest and caught her breath. "A girl killed

20

herself at the center today. I'm heading home now. I was hoping..."

"Oh honey, how horrible! What can I do for you?"

"I was hoping you could come over and have pizza with me and Michael, just hang out for the evening?"

"Yes, you bet. You go home; I'll bring the pizza. See you in about an hour." He clicked off the line.

Dropping the phone in her oversized purse, Maya put the car in gear, and drove through the tree-covered lanes home. She lived only a few blocks from the center in an old part of town, where charming houses full of character lined the narrow streets that welcomed the afternoon walker.

Maya pulled her fifteen-year-old Volvo into the driveway next to her cottage home with a comfortable porch swing to the left of the front door. As soon as she opened the door, Gus, her Australian Shepard, came bounding off the porch to greet her. It was a greeting she welcomed as she buried her face in his and ruffled his fur.

Inside the living room, Michael sat on the couch maneuvering the controls of a video game. He glanced up from the TV. "Hi mom, where's the pizza?"

Maya leaned over and kissed her son on the forehead. "Jon's bringing it."

Gus skidded across the hard wood floors rushing to beat Maya to the kitchen. She tossed a rawhide chew in the air and Gus snatched it mid-flight. She poured herself a large glass of red wine, drank half and topped it off again. She longed for a cigarette, but she'd gone eight days without one and was determined to quit for good this time. She paced the kitchen floor. *There must be a cigarette hidden somewhere*, she thought.

Maya jumped and gasped as the front door slammed. She poked her head around the corner and saw Jon standing in the entry way with two large pizza boxes in one hand, and a six pack of beer in the other. He smiled at her, "Hey honey, it's pizza time."

As Jon passed behind him, Michael tilted his head up to get a good whiff of the pizza, but didn't take his eyes off of the TV. He was nearing his high score, this could be a record-breaking night.

Jon kissed Maya in the kitchen doorway then slid the pizzas on the counter. He stripped a beer from the pack and put the rest in the fridge. He took two long gulps from the can and put his arms around Maya leading her to a chair at the table.

"Sit down, take your shoes off, and let me massage your feet."

Maya's eyes closed and her head sunk into the back of her chair as Jon pushed his thumbs gently up the arch of her right foot. Aching and ecstasy collided in her brain.

"Shall I tell you about my day?" Jon asked.

"Anything to take my mind off mine would be nice." Maya said, as she pulled herself upright for a sip of wine.

Jon slipped his long fingers around Maya's ankle, and gently slid his hands up her calf until her pant leg bunched over her knee. He sensuously massaged the muscles, kissing her leg as he went. He tickled the space behind her knee, causing her to flinch. "I got three new listings in Nampa today, and I'm showing properties to a new buyer tomorrow afternoon. They want something near Lake Lowell."

Maya opened her eyes and sighed, absorbing his strength and energy. His face expressed as much pleasure as she was feeling. "I love you."

He took another swig of beer and rubbed her left foot. "I'm here for you hon, that's all you need to know. I'm here for you."

She closed her eyes again and let her head fall back. She spoke without opening her eyes. "I dreamt about it."

Jon let go of her foot, placed his hands on Maya's thighs and slid them up around her pelvis. He squinted as his hands caressed her in ways that made her squirm. "What?"

Maya leaned forward and placed her hands over his, stopping him. "Two nights ago, I dreamt of a dead girl in the building. Blood encircling her body. I didn't know who it was, or when it would be. But I had the dream." She reached over and took another sip of wine.

"It was just a dream," Jon said dismissively. "It didn't mean it was going to happen."

Maya narrowed her eyes. "When I dream of death, someone dies - every time - Jon." A shadow fell across her green eyes. The wine left a hint of color on her full lips. Jon leaned over and kissed her again, tasting the wine. Cabernet.

Maya brushed Jon's hands away and got up and called out to Michael. "Come on, time to end the game and have some dinner before it gets cold."

Michael and Gus bounded into the kitchen following the aroma of pepperoni and sausage. Every time Maya's thoughts drifted back to Gabriella, she took another sip of wine and gazed into Jon's hazel eyes.

"Spend the night?" Maya whispered into Jon's ear as he finished his last bite of pizza.

"I was planning on it." Jon said as he kissed her forehead, his breath lifting some stray hair around her face.

Michael tossed his paper plate in the trash, washed his last bite of pizza down with a drink of soda, and ignored Jon's embrace of his mother. He placed his glass in the sink. "Hey mom, can I stay over at Charlie's tonight?"

Maya searched Jon's leering eyes. "I suppose, but be home in the morning to take care of Gus."

Michael pushed his way in between her and Jon, and gave his mom a peck on the cheek. "Thanks mom."

Jon's wolfish grin prompted Maya to clear off the table in favor of a more romantic evening. Jon followed her around the kitchen, kissing her shoulders and rubbing his hands over her breasts, stomach, and down to her loins. Maya giggled and squirmed, but fussed at him to give her time to get her work done.

Jon locked the front door, turned off the lights and followed Maya into the bedroom. He pealed her clothes off slowly, covering each patch of bare skin as it was revealed, with his warm lips and wet tongue.

By midnight Maya was exhausted. "Darling," she uttered in a raspy voice, "I have to get some sleep."

Jon kissed her lips, her cheek, and eye lids. "Then sleep for now. I'll finish devouring you later." He smirked as he rolled over.

As tired as she was, Maya couldn't sleep, tossing and turning with images of Gabriella lying in blood on the bathroom floor. *What did she mean by ghosts and demons?*

On Friday morning, Jon had coffee ready before Maya got out of bed. *How does he do it?* She wondered.

Jon waited in his faded red SUV with a bumper sticker over a dent in the front fender that read 'Bite Me!', while Maya got in her car. But the Volvo wouldn't start. She turned the ignition on and off - nothing. She looked up and saw Jon rambling over to her car. She rolled down the window.

"What's the matter?" Jon asked.

"I think the battery must be dead. It won't even turn over."

Jon strode to the front of the car and motioned for her to pop the hood. "Let me take a look." He checked the battery cables and returned to her window. "There's a spark, so it must be something else. Come on, I'll take you to work and we'll figure it out later."

Maya sighed, pulled her things out of her car and got in with Jon. He drove her to the Treasure Valley Counseling Center, and parked in the small parking lot on the east side of the building.

Maya sat and stared at the large stone structure. "You know, I remember when this was still an orphanage - nearly a thousand children a year called this place home. It's not a very welcoming place though, is it?" Her sad eyes glanced over at Jon.

He smiled at her. "Come on now honey, it's a new day and you have a very large center to run. It is welcoming because you work hard to make it that way."

They got out of his SUV and walked to the stone stairway leading to the front door. Maya paused in the middle of the steps.

"I can't get the images of Gabriella out of my mind."

Jon nudged her. "You need to get your mind on work, what's on the agenda today?"

"I'm starting the new marketing campaign for the gala. This could ruin us."

Jon put an arm around her shoulder and pulled her to him. "My darling, you worry too much. The gala is eight months away. Do today's work today. In time everyone will have forgotten about this."

Maya sighed, hoping he was right. *People never forget about death*, she thought as she entered the building. She wondered when she could sneak away for a cigarette.

Gloria, the twenty-something receptionist greeted them with a cheery smile. "Morning Maya, Jon. It's pretty busy for a Friday. I've already had five calls from the paper, TV, and radio stations."

Maya nodded. "I suppose it will be crazy for a while, after yesterday."

Jon elbowed Maya in the side. She smiled up at him. He was nearly a foot taller than Maya, although that wasn't hard, since she was all of four feet and eleven inches. It was why she always wore platform high heels, not because they made her legs look sexy, which didn't hurt, but because she hated being short.

Jon accompanied Maya up the stairs and down the hall to her office. He plopped down on the couch and scrolled through emails on his phone. Maya settled in at her desk and turned on her computer when her phone rang. She went from one call to another, a steady stream of people sharing fears and concerns about Gabriella's death at the center. By ten she was exhausted.

"You don't have to stick around, I'm sure you have work to do." Maya said to Jon.

"It's okay, I don't mind. Besides, I don't need to check into the office for another half hour, then you're on your own, kid."

Maya smiled. "I appreciate it, but right now I need to take a break alone, please." She dug in the back of her desk drawer and felt the cigarette hidden behind the paper clips, she slipped it and a lighter into her pocket and got up from her desk.

"Okay then," Jon said, "I'll head out now and be back in time to take you to lunch." He kissed her on the cheek, then brushed his lips against hers.

I might have to take a breath mint with me too, she thought, since everyone believed she had already quit smoking. It irritated her she couldn't quit, or that she needed to quit. She liked her cigarettes.

Maya snuck out the exit next to her office and wandered through the back yard. She was careful to keep her back to the windows so no one could see her inhale the sweet nicotine and let it fill her lungs. Just one more puff, then a breath mint. She watched a squirrel run through the large pine tree in front of her. It stopped for a moment and looked down at her, shook its tail a few times then scampered up further. The smell of pine reminded her of vacations with her father at the cabin on Cascade Lake.

She remembered squealing as he chased her to the end of the dock. Then she recalled shivering under a tent on a frostbitten morning at his funeral. God, how she missed him. He was her grounding stone. Jon was right, she worried too much, and her mind was constantly filled with chatter. Pine trees, camping, dad, and death. It always came back to death. This was going to ruin the gala, and without a successful gala, the center could lose its funding.

Stop it, she thought to herself. *You're doing it again. Maybe Jon's right, maybe they'll have forgotten about Gabriella by then.* Or maybe she would make a special dedication at next year's gala for Gabriella. That was an idea, use this unfortunate tragedy to rally the troops. Of course! A call to arms, don't let this tragedy be repeated. She took another drag off the cigarette. She was rejuvenated; maybe she could turn this around. Gabriella can't have died in vain.

Her cigarette was nearly done. She rubbed it against the rough stone wall looking around, hoping no one had seen her. A car pulled into the parking lot, a mother and child got out and headed to the front entrance. Maya popped the breath mint into her mouth and headed in the back door. The temperature was creeping up fast. It would be mid-nineties by noon. But the old sandstone building blocked the heat well. Her office was cool and empty.

Jon had gone back to work and Maya was relieved. She loved him, but she had enough to do without having to juggle around him today. Besides, he would smell the cigarette smoke. He was astute like that. *It was irritating.* Maya scrolled through a new batch of emails. She got up and marched to her doorway calling across the hall. "June, please bring me Gabriella Santos' hard file."

Before she got back to her desk, June entered the room with the file in hand. June was ten years Maya's junior, a perky thirty-six year old blond who often wore her teenage daughter's clothes.

"Here you go Maya. Oh, and don't forget, I'm leaving a little early today. I hope that's still okay?"

Maya frowned. "What is it you're doing?"

"Chelsea and I are getting matching tattoos." She giggled and bounced out of the office.

Maya opened the file. "Who gets a matching tattoo with their teenage daughter?" she mumbled.

Maya read through Gabriella's records, searching every entry for clues to indicate suicidal tendencies. But none appeared. No discussions of suicide, no preoccupation with death, no mention of alcohol or drug abuse. None of the normal red flags were raised. She cross-referenced cases, indexed time lines, and highlighted all children in the same foster families.

She wanted another cigarette.

Maya returned to the file summarizing the life of Gabriella. Born in Caldwell, Idaho to a single mother. At age five she was placed into the custody of child protective services after her mother was sent to prison for meth use, and possession with intent to sell. Gabriella had been in a series of foster home placements ever since. She scoured a string of social behavior issues, attitude problems, and diagnosis. Her mother died in prison from drug related complications when Gabriella was seven. No father, no siblings, no family. Yet Maya knew something wasn't being told in the file, and neither she, nor Gabriella, would rest until she found it.

Standing behind her desk, Maya looked out at the tree shaded street below. A sudden breeze pushed through the branches and then disappeared. Stillness settled in on the hot August day. Maya thought about the meth use, it was a common thread in many of the case files at the center. She knew the justifications people gave for drug use, but there were more positive options to overcome problems.

Maya carefully read through all the counseling notes on Gabriella, looking deeper for clues to her death. The notes in her file were so familiar, so similar to other children who entered these doors. She took her reading glasses off, closed her eyes and dropped her face into her hands. The center counseled ninety children a day on average.

Ninety children a day.

The words ran through her mind like a warning. Maya needed to learn from Gabriella to help prevent this for others.

"Speak to me Gabriella." The plea of her heart was barely audible.

A knock on her open door startled her. Jon stood there with his usual grin.

"Hey honey, it's lunch time."

Maya's head slowly shook. "I don't have time for lunch today. Could you just bring me something?"

Jon's eyes narrowed. "How often do you skip lunch, or eat something quick at your desk so you can keep working?"

Maya knew what he was getting at. She rarely took a full lunch break.

"Today's not good, I'm buried here."

Jon gently took her hand and pulled her up. He placed his hands on her shoulders turning her toward him, and looked down into her Irish green eyes. "Maya Sanderson, you are coming with me for an entire hour, away from this place and this work."

Maya took a breath worthy of a dive into the deep end of a swimming pool. She grabbed her purse and let her fiancé rescue her from the dragon that loomed overhead, and lead her out of the room with his arm around her shoulders.

Jon drove to the Sun Rise café on at the east side of town, where they slipped into a booth. Maya let her shoulders relax and her nerves unwind as she enjoyed the chicken and avocado sandwich, but skipped the fries, since she was trying to lose a few pounds. Though he didn't mention it, she could see in Jon's eyes he felt she could be slimmer too. Jon devoured a late breakfast of Belgium waffles and sausage and eggs.

"How's your day going so far?" Maya asked.

"Good. I have an MLS form to fill out this afternoon for a new listing."

Jon washed down his bite with some black coffee. "And I had an offer come in this morning for the Jackson's place; it was a good offer too - just barely under the asking price. There's no way the seller will turn it down. As soon as it closes, I'm taking you out to a nice dinner. We haven't been to the Cottonwood Grill in Boise in a while. Dinner on the patio, a nice bottle of wine, and looking into your eyes - what could be better?"

Jon had proposed to Maya at the Cottonwood Grill. They met in early January when his real estate company sponsored a special winter ball fund raiser for the Center. He asked her to dance, brought her drinks and didn't take his eyes off of her the entire night. It made her nervous at first, but then her heart gave in. He called her the next day to ask her out, and now look at them, eight months later, engaged.

He smiled so sweetly that Maya forgot about Gabriella, the tragedy, and the media, for a moment. She felt only love. Her heart swelled, her mind eased, and she smiled.

"Thank you," Maya said, "thank you for being so wonderful to me."

Jon took her hand and kissed her finger above the small diamond engagement ring, not taking his eyes off of hers. "I love you Maya, I feel what your heart needs and I'm here to fulfill it."

The couple finished lunch and strolled out to Jon's SUV. Before he opened Maya's door, he wrapped his arms around her waist, lifted her up against the car, and kissed her, intermingling the Belgian waffle and the chicken avocado in a burst of passion. Maya slid down out of his arms, but not out of his lips. His hands glided up to her neck and face, slipping through her hair, as he savored the taste of her breath, her mouth, her perfume.

Maya's heart raced, her chest heaved, and her legs felt a sudden impulse to wrap around him. Her mind reeled with desire. She drew herself out of his embrace.

"I have to get back to the office," she whispered.

Jon brushed his tongue over her bottom lip. "We could go down to the basement. It's dark down there. No one would know."

Maya nervously laughed. "Don't be silly."

Jon winked at Maya and opened her door. He brushed her thigh as she scooted onto the seat. He drove her back to the center and put the truck in park without turning the ignition off. "Hon, I should be in the office the rest of the day. I have some work to do on my new listings. If you need anything, you call me, promise?"

Maya opened her door to get out. "Okay, but I'll be fine."

Jon grabbed her left hand as she slid off the seat to the gravel parking lot. "Call me when you're done - I'll give you a ride, and take another look at your car."

"No worries, I called the mechanic this morning. They were going to look at it today. Besides, I want to walk home tonight, I could use the exercise. I'll talk to you later."

Jon leaned on the window of the SUV, all smiles as usual. It annoyed her, but most things annoyed her these days. She waited to watch him leave the parking lot. He blew her a kiss and put the vehicle in reverse. She stared at the empty space between the two of them, where the kiss lingered and eventually fell.

Late afternoon found Maya leaning against the back of the building, enjoying the shade of the trees, and the satisfying nicotine of another cigarette. She released a puff of smoke which drifted up and comingled with the low hanging branch of a tree. She analyzed the cigarette in her hand. She realized she was going to have to quit, for real, before the wedding. Jon paid close attention to her, unlike her ex-husband Jake. She could have run a chainsaw under Jake's nose and he wouldn't have noticed she was in the room.

She rubbed the cigarette out on a rock and headed back in to finish up the day.

It was nearly six o'clock when Maya looked at her watch and decided she better head home. Her phone whistled with a text. It was from Jon.

"Sure you don't need a ride?"

"No, I want the walk." She texted back.

Maya turned her computer off, packed up to head home and locked the doors and the day's work behind her. She strolled down 12th Avenue, then over to Albany Street toward her home on Belmont.

Maya relished the transition of life from work to home. The counseling center was a century-old building of sandstone walls that were unforgiving, obstructing light and hoarding darkness. Crossing the street she left the dark forest and entered the meadow. Strolling along the neighborhood sidewalks, she enjoyed the bursts of sunlight as they pierced through the branches she passed under. Children playing, families on bicycles, friends sitting on their porches drinking and laughing. The path from work to home was relaxing and invigorating, reminding her of the value of simplicity.

As Maya crossed to Belmont, she saw Jon's SUV parked in front of her house. Her stomach knotted and cramped. She stopped for a moment bending over and holding her large purse in front of her to put pressure on the pain. It eased up enough for her to continue home.

Michael was sitting on the couch playing his video game, when Maya entered the living room.

"Hi," Michael said, without taking his eyes off of the screen. A bag of chips sat crumpled and scattered on the couch beside him, and Gus lay at his feet. The dog raised his eyes to greet Maya, but the heat had gotten to him too.

"Don't worry," Maya said as she passed through the living room, "I'll fix some dinner. I can see you're too busy."

Jon came out of the bathroom and scooted the bag of chips over and sat down on the couch with Michael. "Play you a game?" he asked.

Michael glanced over, one raised eyebrow. "You play Halo?"

Jon smirked. "Are you kidding? Step aside kid and watch a pro!"

Michael reset the console, added Jon, and handed him a controller.

Standing in the kitchen looking in the refrigerator, Maya glanced at the two guys in the living room, glued to the flat screen. It was late, hot, and she was tired. Her eyes lit up at the dish of left over lasagna on the bottom shelf. She smiled and pulled it out.

"Left overs for dinner tonight. It's in the microwave, and it's self-serve!" Maya fixed herself a plate, poured a glass of red wine, and sat down at the table, kicking her shoes off and putting her feet up on the chair across from her. She took a bite of lasagna, washed it down with the smooth Cabernet, taking time to savor the flavors. The pasta, the basil, the ricotta cheese, the grapes and all the herbs. Life was bursting in her mouth.

Jon ambled in and poured himself a glass of wine.

"When did you get here?" Maya asked trying to hide the twinge in her gut.

"I got done early so I thought I'd surprise you. I arrived about an hour ago." He leaned over her, dragging his tongue from her ear down her neck.

Maya twitched at the sensation and fidgeted. She leaned back in her chair and looked up at him.

"Are you staying tonight?"

Jon sat down next to her, took her left hand in his and kissed each finger one by one. "No," he said, "I have some things to do this evening before I head out of town." He winked at her and got up.

"Oh right, you have that training in Coeur d'Alene this weekend." Maya said.

Jon rolled his eyes. "Yep, real estate continuing education. Boring. But I'll be home Sunday."

"You can be bored, but I'll be busy. I have plenty to do this weekend."

Jon kissed her on the forehead and high-fived Michael as he strolled through the living room. "Great game, kid!" The front screen door slammed behind him.

Michael joined his mom in the kitchen and cleared off the table as she placed a stopper in the wine bottle. He put the last dirty dish in the dishwasher and wiped his hands off on a towel. She looked at him with suspicious eyes.

"What has gotten into you?" Maya asked smiling.

"What do you mean?"

"This helpful side of you, I like it. But it's not normal. What are you up to?"

Michael shrugged, something he was good at.

"I don't know. Jon said you had a rough day at work, needed a little help. So I helped. But I'm going over to the skate park with Charlie, so the rest of the house is up to you," he said, flashing the cheesy grin that made Maya laugh since he was a toddler.

"Do you have your stuff packed and ready to go for tomorrow morning?"

Michael grimaced. "Do I have to go? I always feel so awkward at Grandma's."

Maya smiled at her son. "Hon, your grandma loves you, and she doesn't get to see you very much. You'll have a good weekend."

Michael turned back around and headed into his bedroom. "I hate going to Utah."

"After everything's packed then you can go to the skate park." Maya called out to him.

Maya uncorked the wine, refilled her glass, and pulled a cigarette and a paperback book out of her purse. She ambled out onto the back porch and eased into the Adirondack chair. She reveled in the sparrow's songs from the large trees sheltering her with a cool shade.

Maya sipped her wine and read her book for three hours until her eyelids got heavy. She slid a book marker in between the pages, and took her empty glass into the kitchen, making her way to the bedroom.

That night, as Maya snuggled into her queen size bed, the breezes filtering through the window screen echoed whispers as she drifted off to sleep.

"Speak to me Gabriella."

42

SHERRY BRISCOE

Maya traveled through dark passages following a flicker of light that bounced back and forth. She felt anxious, unsettled. Each time she reached her hand out to help her find her way, she was paralyzed with fear. Then she stood barefoot on the lawn in front of the counseling center. The grass felt cool and damp beneath her feet, it tickled her toes. The moon was bright above her and a breeze pushed its way through the trees brushing her cheek and the long night shirt she was wearing. Gabriella stood on the steps, holding her hand out to Maya.

"There's something you need to know." The spirit said, without moving her mouth.

Maya struggled to move to the century old building, her legs feeling as heavy as if they were weighted down with cement blocks. When she reached the first step, Gabriella stood in the doorway, signaling for Maya to follow her, and mouthing soundless words.

"What is it? What are you saying, Gabriella?" Maya called out. The lobby was dark and empty, and Gabriella stood in the hallway, waiting for Maya to join her. She turned to the right. A cardboard box sat on the floor with a worn book sitting on top of it.

Maya bolted upright to the blare of her alarm clock, then cursed it for interrupting.

43

It was a dream. She thought. *A dream that seemed so real.* She sat on the edge of her bed and stretched, feeling the creeks and stiffness leave her body. Her feet slid into her slippers and she shuffled into the bathroom.

Maya stood in her shower, the hot water beating on her face and chest. Her eyes closed, straining to remember the dream. Was there anything else? Gabriella had gone through the lobby and turned right. But they'd found her in the restroom which was to the left. Maya turned to let the water drench her red hair, pound into her neck, shoulders and cascade down her back.

What's to the right? Maya wondered.

Maya made coffee and called out as she passed Michael's bedroom door. "You better be getting ready to go soon."

She opened the front door to let the dog out and stepped onto the front porch to get the morning paper. She waited in the porch swing while Gus relieved himself on the neighbor's oak tree. The dog exchanged sniffs with the neighbor's boxer then returned to the porch by Maya. Finished with their outside tasks, they went back in the house.

Maya headed for the kitchen and Gus ran into Michael's bedroom. Maya smiled, *it's about time you got up*, she thought. Her poppy seed bagel popped up from the toaster. She slathered it generously with cream cheese, sat down at the table with the paper, the bagel and her coffee in hand.

"Michael, you better hurry and get ready. Your dad will be here in about an hour." She pulled a pencil out of a box of pens and pencils on the table, as she read through the crossword puzzle.

Michael stumbled into the kitchen rubbing his eyes. "What time is it?"

"It's time for you to get ready. Have a bagel if you want, you'll need something before you guys leave town."

After Jake picked up Michael, Maya sat on the front porch swing, with Gus resting at her feet.

"Well this is going to be great." Maya said to Gus. "A weekend alone. I should get all kinds of things accomplished. Besides working on performance evaluations, grant paperwork, and board meeting reports, I can also do laundry and housework." She put a Joni Mitchell CD into the stereo, turned the volume up, and danced her way through a day of chores.

After lunch the mechanic called. Maya took Gus for a walk to the shop to pick up the car. It was odd they couldn't find anything wrong with it, but it was running fine now. Saturday evening Maya treated herself to a movie. She inserted her DVD of Titanic, popped a large bowl of popcorn, and she and Gus settled in for an evening of romance on a cold ocean liner. As the credits at the end of the movie rolled across the screen, Gus licked the empty popcorn bowl clean. Maya's cell phone rang.

"Hello, how's north Idaho?" she asked.

"It would be better with you here," Jon said on the other end.

Maya let out a sigh of happiness. "Gus and I are enjoying our solitude."

"It's beautiful up here, but I can't wait to get home to you. So what are you wearing? Anything?" Jon asked.

Maya giggled. She finished the conversation, turned off the lights and she and Gus went to bed.

Sunday was yard work, cleaning floors and windows, and spending a few more hours on her laptop with leftover work from the office. She also managed to season some chicken breasts and have them ready to be barbequed as soon as Jon got home.

Monday morning came too soon, but she was happy Michael would be home later that afternoon. She threw the morning paper into her bag to read at the office, giving her time to stop at the coffee shop on her way in.

Sitting at her desk, with a chai latte, Maya flipped through the paper until her focus and hands froze on the death notices. GABRIELLA SANTOS of Boise, born April 5, 2001, died August 3, 2015. Arrangements pending. *That's it?* Maya wondered. No mention of her mother, her inspiring poems she had written for the counselors over the past four years, and her excitement two years ago when she received a top student award at school for her high grades in literature. Maya smiled at the memory of Gabriella bouncing into her office one afternoon to show off the award.

Maya was seized with a gaping emptiness in her heart, a dark void cried out for some acknowledgement of the young woman who took her own life. Gabriella lived, that was far more important than the fact she died.

Maya went downstairs to the first floor and knocked on Sandy's door. "Got a minute?"

Sandy waved her in. "Of course, Maya, what can I do for you?"

"I know we've already discussed Gabriella's files, and the lack of any warning signs of suicidal behavior. But I was wondering if you noticed anything in her behavior over the past two years to indicate a change in her? Anything about school or home life, maybe not a red flag,

FORGOTTEN LIVES: *Where Evil Lurks*

but a subtle sign of something different?" Maya wanted to understand.

Sandy shook her head. "I've poured over my notes on her. I feel like I missed something I should have seen. But I'm telling you, there's nothing there."

Maya bit her lower lip, shifted her gaze to the carpeting, then back to Sandy. "I keep getting the feeling there is a clue somewhere, I just don't know where yet."

Sandy shook her head. "If I find anything, you'll be the first to know."

June caught Maya in the hallway. "Maya, I need you to approve these receipts, and you have the Simplot grant application due today."

Maya headed back to her office. Her search for answers would have to wait. She had a center to keep afloat for now.

Like most Mondays, this one was no different with Maya feeling like a smoke jumper, plunging from one fire to another. As the day wore on, the flames turned into a wisp of smoke from a smoldering ember. It would wait until tomorrow. She looked at her watch, it was four-thirty and she wanted to get home to meet Michael. She packed up her things and headed home.

The house was empty when Maya got home at five o'clock. "Michael!" No answer. She hurried through the house and onto the back porch. Gus was lying under a tree in the corner of the back yard, but there was no sign of Michael yet. Gus bounded for the back porch wagging his tail, excited to see his master home.

"Where's Michael?" Maya asked, but the dog didn't answer. She walked back into the house and pulled out her cell phone. As she was getting ready to dial Michael's phone, the front door opened, with Michael and Jon walked in together.

Maya strolled into the living room and hugged her son. "I'm glad you're home. Did you have fun?"

Michael frowned. "It was Utah, mom."

"I thought you were supposed to be home an hour ago. What have you two been up to?" She looked up at Jon for an explanation.

"Jon was here when dad dropped me off, so we went for some ice cream. No big deal," Michael said.

Jon shrugged. "Sorry, honey, I didn't expect you home so early. I was thinking of taking you both out to dinner tonight. Anyone want Mexican?"

Maya kissed her son's forehead and gave him another squeeze before she let go. "Mexican sounds good to me."

49

On Tuesday morning life around the Sanderson home was back to normal. Michael staggered into the kitchen rubbing his eyes. "What's for breakfast?"

Maya folded the paper, took the last bite of her bagel and stood up to hug her son. "Whatever you can find dear, I have to get to work. Please be sure to clean up after yourself, and don't forget to feed Gus. You only have three weeks of freedom left before school starts, I suggest you use your time wisely." She kissed him on the forehead and put her empty coffee cup in the sink.

"Why are you so cheery this morning?" Michael looked at her bewildered. He swatted at Gus, who was tugging on his oversized tee shirt.

Maya smiled. "Because of you, Michael. Because I am blessed with such a wonderful son, and I'm glad you're home. But don't forget to change your sheets, tomorrow's laundry day." She winked at him, grabbed her bag and headed out the door.

Michael shrugged and pulled the sack of dog food out of the pantry.

When Maya arrived at work and entered her office, she was greeted by a cardboard box on the floor in front of her desk. She turned to find June standing in the doorway.

"What's this?" Maya asked.

June leaned against the door jam, her arms folded across her chest. "Gabriella's foster parents took it to Gabriella's social worker at Health and Welfare."

"Oh, my friend, Betty." Maya said.

"It's all of Gabriella's possessions. The family kept her clothes, they said their older daughter could wear them. Betty said she wanted you to go through it first."

Maya looked at the box and then at June. "Only Betty would do that. I wonder what it is she thinks I'll find?"

June pursed her lips and shrugged. "I don't know. Let me know if you need anything else."

Maya viewed the box. "No thanks, this is fine."

June went back to her office. Maya pulled the box over to the couch and sat down. She slowly removed the lid and there on top of everything else was the book from her dream. It was Gabriella's journal. Her hand trembled as she reached for it. She exhaled as she stared at the worn journal. She got up and marched over to her desk, slid open the drawer to get a cigarette, snatched the journal from the box and scurried down the side stairs and out the door into the back yard.

Gabriella's handwriting was tiny but neat. She wrote words of a tortured soul, unwanted and unloved, who could still dream and want to love. She described the caterpillar trapped in her limiting cocoon, and how she ached to spread her wings and fly above the darkness she feared. She felt evil all around her, but saw a shimmer from an Angel's wings in the far off horizon. She wanted so much to touch the glistening white feathers of God's perfect ones.

Maya's heart ached more with each page she read. Her eyes filled with tears at the pain and abuse inflicted on this fragile girl.

Gabriella wrote of the foster parents who locked her in her room, barely fed her, and beat her. She wrote of boys she would run away with, the temptations of drugs, and alcohol. She wrote of the tall man who followed her out of the counseling center one day and raped her. He did not work there, but she had seen him in the halls. On the last page of her journal, she wrote this entry:

The counseling center
Used to be my refuge,
they are the only ones who care.
But a dark stranger follows me there.
His voice is kind but his words are rough.
For him, taking my body is not enough.
Because of him, I must die,
I cannot tell you why.

Not yet.

On the last page, Gabriella had scribbled her final words:

Sacrifice is not wrong

If it is the only way

To save God's Angel.

Maya clutched the book to her chest and rushed back up to her office. She threw the journal on her desk and rummaged through the rest of the items in the box, but there was nothing else to explain who this man was, and what he had to do with Gabriella's death. Panic surged through her entire body. She had to discover who the dark stranger was before more kids were hurt. She felt helpless as she stared at the journal with faded pages.

"Who was he?" She asked.

"Who was who?" Jon said, standing in her doorway.

Maya was startled and rubbed at her eyes. She'd forgotten to pop a breath mint or some gum in her mouth. Jon would smell the cigarette, she couldn't let him near her. "Oh nothing, just thinking out loud. I didn't expect to see you here today."

"Just stopping by on my way to sign up a listing. The Cunningham Mansion across the street is going on the market. Can you believe it? That place is so amazing. We should buy it." He winked at her.

Maya dug in her purse and found a stick of Juicy Fruit gum, shoved it in her mouth and forced a smile. "The Cunningham mansion? Jon, I don't want to live in a house that's over a hundred years old. I fight with the age of this building enough as it is. Besides, I like my house. I don't want to move."

Jon laughed. "Okay, okay. I was kidding, Maya. But you should come over with me and see the inside. It has a very medieval feel to it."

Maya slipped the journal into her desk drawer. "I've been in that house, it's not my taste. You go ahead. I have a ton of work to get done." She sat down and pulled a file off of the stack on the corner of her desk.

Jon strolled over, stood behind her, and rubbed her shoulders. "Babe, you are really tight. What's wrong?"

Maya rolled her shoulders and then her neck. "Like I said, I just have a lot of work."

"Okay, I can take a hint. I'll get out of your hair. Come on, you can at least walk me out to my car." He grabbed her hand and led her to the door. She chewed her gum as they made their way out of the building, hoping he wouldn't smell the cigarette smoke on her.

They stood on the large cement steps in the front of the building. Maya paused on the top step and noticed a butterfly flitter between them and land on the side railing.

"I have to pick up some things on the way home tonight. How about I call you later?" Maya asked.

Jon forcefully wrapped his arms around her and pulled her chest into his, pushing his tongue deep in her mouth. His breath was hot and there was a strange taste. A bitterness she didn't recognize.

Maya tried to pull away from Jon, but he held her tighter, one hand behind her head, his mouth enveloping hers. She could hardly breathe.

Jon released her with a disturbing smile. She staggered back a step unsure of what just happened. She wiped her mouth of the unpleasant taste, and glanced over to see the butterfly dead on the rail.

A family came up the steps. Maya caught Jon leering at Melissa, a nine year old girl coming in with her parents. Melissa grabbed her mother's arm and pulled it around her, peeking wide-eyed back at Jon.

Maya's heart pounded and her head began to spin. She felt ill and thought she might vomit on the stairs. She grabbed the rail to steady herself, closed her eyes for a moment and caught her breath. When she opened them Jon was standing at the bottom of the stairs, smiling and waving at her, seemingly unaware she had almost collapsed in front of him.

Maya felt chilled and wrapped her arms around herself despite the hot summer day. She went back up to her office, and shut the door. She pulled out Gabriella's journal and read through it again.

"Speak to me Gabriella. Who was the tall stranger? Why did you have to die?"

The phone rang and Maya jumped, caught her breath, and answered. "Treasure Valley Counseling Center, this is Maya. Hi Betty, I got Gabriella's box, and thank you. What? Of course I would, send it over. Thanks." June knocked on the door and entered as soon as Maya hung up the phone. "Betty ended up with Gabriella's backpack too, so she's sending it over."

"I suppose it's good to keep it all together. Well, I've got the Medicaid billing done, and the schedules for the counselors set. The new marketing gal wanted to know if you were available this afternoon to talk about the gala. What should I tell her?"

Maya took a drink of her coffee and collected her thoughts. "I'm here all day. Sure, that's fine."

June started to close the door.

"Leave it open, June. Thanks."

June smiled and went back to her office.

Maya opened the window behind her desk to let in some fresh air. She wondered what made her feel ill. She shook her head and pulled in a deep breath. *I have to get back to work*, she thought. She forced the image on the front steps aside. She had a gala to organize, a center to run, and when there was time, a wedding to plan, she reminded herself.

Two nights later Gabriella visited Maya in her dreams again. From the hallway, Maya followed the spirit of the young girl to the exit at the end of the hall. The image of Gabriella moved in a fragmented motion across the lawn to a small building on the corner of the block. Maya followed the spirit into the vacant house and down the narrow steps to the musty basement.

Gabriella's white hand pointed to an old mattress on the cold cement floor in the corner.

"Woof!" Maya was awakened by a hungry Gus staring her straight in the face. Their noses touched.

"Good morning to you too, Gus. Go wake up Michael, he can let you out today." Maya rolled over and pulled the pillow over her head. She peeked at the clock beside her bed. She could rest for another ten minutes, but then she had to get up and get ready for work.

When Maya walked in the door at the center, phones were ringing, the lobby was filled with the chatter of children waiting to see the counselors, and staff buzzed like bees in spring. Maya smiled. They *were* making a positive difference in people's lives.

Maya added some water to the bouquet of flowers Jon sent her the day before. They were a fragrant reminder of how much he would miss her while he was in Vegas for three days at a real estate convention. He seemed to travel a lot, she thought. She smiled at the yellow roses nestled into a spray of white daisies.

The phone rang and business continued.

It was two-thirty when Maya had time to pull a left over tomato bisque soup from the refrigerator and microwave it for two minutes. She was carrying it back to her office when she ran into Jon at the top of the stairs.

"Hey gorgeous." He smiled at her. "Did you miss me?"

"Of course, but I thought you weren't coming home until tomorrow." She smiled. He kissed her on the lips, then the neck making her squirm. "Hey I've got hot soup in my hands."

"We got done early. I'm heading across the street to the Cunningham Mansion to meet a prospective buyer, how about I stop back later when you aren't armed and dangerous?" He gave her a look causing her to melt, with or without summer heat.

"I'd like that. See you later."

Jon kissed her, dragging his tongue across her lips, sucking her in. He wanted more – and Maya knew it when she saw him, she was a thirst that was never quenched with him. Maya nudged him aside and placed her soup bowl on the desk. He stepped back, smiled and strolled down the hall, waving at June as he passed her office.

"Later, ladies," Jon said as he took the final steps toward the door to the back stairs.

Maya sat down and sipped her soup as she delved back into the pile of work on her desk. She got through half the stack in just under two hours. She felt she deserved a reward. She opened her drawer, and pulled out a cigarette from her secret stash. *I earned you today*, she thought.

Stepping out the side door of the building into the midday sun, Maya squinted into the harsh brightness. A small group of children played in the yard behind the building, so she strolled out to the sidewalk trying to find a spot she could smoke without being seen. There were so many people out enjoying the day. She continued to the north corner of the block and saw the house Gabriella showed her in the dream. It seemed empty, but there was no sign indicating it was for-sale or rent. The lawn was dry and full of weeds. She peered in the windows.

Vacant.

Maya meandered around to the back door and reached out to the knob.

Unlocked.

Slowly Maya turned the knob and eased the door open. The rooms were bare with a thick layer of dust on the surfaces. She leaned against the kitchen counter and lit up her cigarette. She exhaled and just as she started to take another drag, she heard a muffled sound emanating from the basement. It sounded like grunting and a child struggling. She took off her shoes and silently crept across the dusty floor to the doorway of the dark, narrow stairs leading down. Her heart pounded harder and faster with each beat. She prayed to God she would not find anything. She gulped, and with right foot on the tread, then left, descended into the darkness, one stride at a time.

A step creaked.

Maya stopped and held her breath. She listened to the rustling sounds that continued, unaware of her presence.

She took another step.

Movement caught her eye in the corner of the dim room, but it took a minute for her eyes to adjust to the dark. A ray of light filtered through a small window at the top of the wall exposing a man humping an unidentifiable person beneath him, on the mattress on the floor. With every thrust he grunted and the frail voice of a girl let out a muffled cry. Maya's heart caught in her throat as she gasped. The man thrust a final push and groaned with release as his body eased, he turned.

The light from the window revealed two red eyes.

Maya's heart nearly exploded. The demon! She backed up into the wall horrified. He pulled himself out of the girl and cast her aside. The girl cried and wiggled to get away from him. He stood and turned toward the stairs.

Maya closed her eyes not wanting to look into his haunting eyes again. She opened her eyes and saw him stare at her. His eyes didn't glow anymore, but she couldn't tell who he was.

"Maya, what are you doing here?" Jon called down to her from the top of the stairs.

Tears streamed from her eyes and her body shook, Maya looked up at Jon, then over at the girl. But the man in the basement was gone. The girl curled into a fetal position and whimpered.

Maya's eyes searched the darkness but saw only the shape of the girl. She rushed down the last two steps and across the cold room. She fell to her knees and grabbed the girl, turning her over to see her face in the tiny bit of light. Her mouth was gagged and her hands were tied behind her. Maya quickly untied the dirty strips of cloth, found her panties, and helped her up.

"Oh my God, Melissa?"

Melissa sobbed and plunged her face into Maya's chest.

"Where did he go?" Maya asked as she looked around the small room.

"Who?" Jon asked as he started down the stairs.

"There was a man, he was just here." She looked up at Jon. "What are you doing here?"

Jon stood at the bottom stair and looked across the small room to Melissa huddled in Maya's arms. "I was looking for you. You bring her up, I'll go outside and see if I can see anyone."

She wiped her eyes and brushed Melissa's hair out of her face. The air was cold. She looked back up at Jon. He smiled, turned, and hiked up the stairs taking two steps at a time.

How could he have vanished so quickly? Her head was swimming. Her body shook with fear.

Maya sat on the floor and folded her arms around Melissa and rocked. Both of them cried.

"You're safe now."

Melissa sniffled and looked up into Maya's eyes. "He's here for you. That's what he said."

Maya pulled back, a sense of horror surging through her veins. "What do you mean? Who is here for me?"

Melissa became suddenly still, her sobbing halted. She shook her head. "He was just on the steps."

Maya's heart skipped a beat, maybe even two. She looked to the empty stairs.

How could I be so blind, she wondered? Her heart seized. Her entire body wept.

Clutching the girl tight to her chest, Maya carried Melissa out of the building and over to the Center.

"Call 911. And find Melissa's parents," Maya said as she rushed in the lobby.

Amy, the bookkeeper, quickly wrapped the sweater from the back of her chair around Melissa. Maya took Melissa into one of the empty counseling rooms and held her until her parents arrived.

The police arrived just minutes before Melissa's mother rushed into the building. They all converged on Maya and the girl. Melissa's mother snatched the girl out of Maya's hands and fell into a chair holding her.

A female officer with a name tag of Nielsen took out her note pad and sat down across from Maya. "Can you tell me what transpired?"

Patrick, a male officer spoke to Melissa's mother. "Where was your daughter before this happened?" he asked.

The mother's tears fell into Melissa's hair. "She was playing with her friends. We only live a few blocks from here."

Paramedics came in and got a stretcher ready to transport Melissa to the hospital.

"Has there been anyone lurking around the neighborhood lately? Any suspicious characters?" Patrick asked.

Melissa's mother cried angry tears. "I don't know."

Officer Nielsen wrote in her pad. "Was there anyone else there?" she asked Maya.

"Jon, my fiancé." Maya said. "He was on the stairs." She felt suffocated, something was pushing against her chest.

"And what was he doing there?" Officer Nielsen asked.

Maya shook her head. "I don't know. He was just there." She gave the officer all of Jon's information along with her own.

Maya staggered up the stairs to her office, her legs aching with each stride, her chest heaving with each breath. She couldn't calm down. She sat at her desk with her door shut and wept.

The day seemed to drag in slow motion until five o'clock when the staff closed up for the night. Maya stood in her office looking out the window with her arms wrapped around herself. She felt sick. Her phone rang.

"Treasure Valley Counseling Center, this is Maya. Detective Hardy, yes of course I remember you. Jon? No, I haven't seen him since this afternoon. What do you mean he doesn't seem to exist?"

She listened as she became more frightened with each word. "He works for...But I've seen his... Yes, I understand. Thank you." Maya slowly hung up the phone and slumped into her chair. "Who in the hell is he?" Her jaw tightened with fury as she took her engagement ring off and threw it against the wall.

"He's here for me," Maya muttered. She jumped out of her chair wild-eyed. "My God, Michael!"

Maya turned the lights off, locked the doors behind her as she exited the large building. She drove straight home.

Maya rushed in the front door to a quiet house. "Michael!" she called out.

No answer.

Maya hurried into the back yard, but he wasn't there either. Neither was Gus. *Maybe Michael took Gus for a walk?* She thought. She pulled out her cell phone to text him as the phone rang. It was Michael. She felt relieved.

"Hello." The other end was silent for a moment. "Michael?"

"Mom?" Michael's voice wash shaky. Maya's heart caught in her throat.

"Michael, what's wrong? Where are you?"

"Mom," he sniffed. "I'm okay."

"Michael! Where are you?" Maya screamed into the cell phone.

Jon's voice came on. "He's with me. I'll take good care of him as long as you do what I say."

Maya collapsed onto the couch. "What do you want?" she asked icily.

"I want you. Now listen to me very carefully…"

Maya dropped the phone into her lap when the call ended, and sat motionless as her mind grappled to comprehend what she needed to do. She was in shock. Michael was in the hands of a madman, a demon. She fumbled through her purse, then bent down and dumped its contents on the coffee table, searching frantically through makeup, papers and her wallet.

Detective Ray Hardy's business card was in a stack of cards. She fumbled and dropped them all on the floor. She pushed the others aside and pick up the detective's.

Maya struggled to read the number, as her hand shook. She dialed. "Hello, this is Maya Sanderson."

"Yes, what can I do for you?" His voice was as soothing as she remembered.

"I need your help." She broke down in tears, sniffling between words.

"Calm down, take it easy and tell me what's happened."

"Jon has my son. Yes, the man you couldn't find anything on. He's taken my son and is holding him hostage. He wants me."

Ten minutes later Ray Hardy was standing at her doorway. She ushered him into her living room and sat down across from him on the couch. She shared the terrifying message she had been given. It wasn't Gabriella who was meant to die, it was Maya. Now it was her, or Michael.

Detective Hardy scribbled notes on a small pad as he listened.

Maya sat in a daze remembering Gabriella's final words:

Sacrifice is not wrong
If it is the only way
To save God's Angel.

"Maybe there is no way out. Maybe this *is* something I have to do." Maya's voice was filled with defeat. She tried to form a rational thought, but her mind was swimming in a pool of fear.

Detective Hardy looked up at her. "Mrs. Sanderson, you can't."

Maya offered a shallow smile. "Call me Maya. I haven't been married for nine years." She sat looking out the window, and a strange calm came over her as tears rolled down her cheeks. "Please take me to the exchange spot. Bring Michael back here and have him call his father." She had thought it out. There was no way to get around the deal Jon offered. Only one of them could live, and it would be Michael.

"Maya, he's given you until eleven p.m. I'll get a team together and hash out a plan. This is my job now."

Turning her eyes to the floor, Maya nodded. "I can't let my son die."

"Of course you can't, but I can't knowingly let him kill you, either." Detective Hardy got on his cell phone. "I need the Watch Commander. This is Hardy. I have a kidnapping hostage situation, assemble the team and I'll be right there." He ended the call and looked at Maya. "Why don't you follow me, we need to meet my team at the station."

Maya drove her car to the police station six blocks away. All she could think about was her son. Her world had been reduced to one person – Michael.

Inside the station she sat in a daze, nursing a cup of coffee as officers plotted and planned to intervene with Jon's plans, and save her son. She understood this was no ordinary criminal, this was evil incarnate. There was no way to fool him or capture him.

Is everything in order? She wondered. *My bills are all caught up, my will is written. I could write a note to Michael, but he wouldn't understand. Sacrifice isn't wrong, if it saves an Angel.* Her chest felt like it was collapsing under a hundred pound cement block.

Detective Hardy sat down beside her. "How are you holding up?"

Maya tried to smile, but it wasn't sincere. "As well as can be expected."

"I've got a couple of snipers that are going out now to scout the area and position themselves out of sight. We want to be ready before he gets there."

"Snipers?" Maya sniffled.

"They will be there for protection." Detective Hardy assured her.

It was ten-thirty, time to head up to the meeting point Jon had given. A dirt road above Arrowrock Dam, east of Boise. Maya got in her Volvo and lit up a cigarette as she slid in her favorite James Taylor CD. Detective Hardy and two unmarked police cars following close behind as they headed east out of town.

Maya drove onto the narrow gravel road above the reservoir that followed the edge of the water. She parked her car and got out. The stars filled the sky above them like diamond drops. She was careful not to get too close to the edge. It was a long drop off to the water below. She gulped. She marched to the firing squad that lay ahead. She lit another cigarette and smoked it along the way.

No point in hiding it now.

Three police cars had parked up the road earlier, and the officers were staked out in critical positions. Detective Hardy drove up behind Maya, but turned off his lights and parked farther back so as not to be seen. There was not much room to maneuver in this spot. Jon had planned it well.

"Michael!" Maya called out.

Jon appeared in the middle of the road in front of her. "Michael's safe." He held Michael in front of him like a shield. Michael's wrists were tied behind his back, and he had a scarf tied around his head, covering his eyes.

Maya stood there motionless for a moment, remembering what Detective Hardy told her. She called out to Jon. "Let Michael go and I'll come to you."

Jon sneered. "When I have you here in my grasp, Michael is free to go."

"Bastard!" Maya said under her breath. She took a step forward.

She repeated Detective Hardy's coaching in her mind. *Don't go all the way. Snipers will be in position. They'll shoot if necessary.*

Maya blinked her eyes. She took another wavering step. She thought about the events about to unfold with each slow and steady stride in the loose gravel. She was halfway there. She couldn't see any snipers, but she trusted they were out there.

"But I don't care," Maya muttered to herself. "I will die as long as Michael lives."

"Is this the choice you want to make?" a soft, childlike voice said.

Maya stopped, her heart raced, and her body trembled. *I want my son back*, she thought.

Maya saw a shimmer in her peripheral vision. She glanced for just a second. "Gabriella?" She whispered.

The spirit of the young girl smiled at Maya.

Maya dropped to her knees and sobbed. "I don't want anyone to die."

As she fell onto the gravel, a shot pierced the evening silence and everyone scrambled. Maya looked up to see Michael on his knees in front of her. She lunged forward and wrapped her arms around him. She pulled the scarf off of his head and kissed his eyes.

"Are you okay? Are you hurt?" she cried out.

Michael smiled and laid his head against her chest. "I'm okay Mom, I'm okay."

The hillside and road were lit up with flood lights and flashlights as officers converged from every direction. They searched the SUV, the road and the hillside, looking for Jon.

But they found no one.

Even the water below was still with not so much as a ripple in the moonlight.

Maya sat in the gravel holding onto her son, crying. Detective Hardy helped them both up and signaled paramedics to assist them.

August was ushered in on the sharp edge of a razor blade, and escaped with unanswered questions. The police never found Jon. When they went to his apartment it was empty and cleaned, leaving no clues to his identity or whereabouts. His faded red SUV was hauled to the impound.

Maya sat on her back porch with an evening breeze stroking the gentle leaves in the trees, sipping her wine, smoking a cigarette. She wasn't ready to quit.

Not yet.

Maya's peaceful evening was interrupted by a man standing in her yard next to the fence under the large oak tree. A warning sensation hurdled down her back. She stood up to see who he was, but on second glance he was gone. *Where did he go?*

She sat back down and took a drink of wine. *I must have imagined it*, she thought.

Michael came out on the deck. "Hey mom, I'm heading over to the skate park."

"Don't stay out too late," Maya said.

"I won't. Oh yeah, I was going to tell you someone must have bought Jon's SUV, I saw it drive by earlier this afternoon."

A nauseating chill rushed over Maya, she glanced up and Michael. "It couldn't be his, it's in the impound."

"It was his, had the same dent in the fender with his bumper sticker over it."

"Who was driving?" Maya was almost afraid to ask.

Michael shrugged. "I couldn't see, just some guy with funky red sunglasses." He leaned down and gave his mom a peck on the cheek and let the screen door slam behind him.

Maya's fingers quavered as she took a drag of her cigarette. Her eyes darted along the fence of her back yard. She hadn't imagined it, he was out there. He wouldn't leave until he got what he came for.

"I still have a few tricks up my sleeve too." Maya murmured to the shadows that slipped through the trees. "This isn't over. Not yet."

ISABELLA

The Healer

September in eastern Oregon was dry and hot. Dogs panted with their tongues hanging out, and cats retreated to cool shady spots in the tall grass, as children ran through sprinklers. Isabella stood on her back porch in the early morning, taking advantage of the quiet time before clients arrived. She reached out and placed a hand on the corner post, closed her eyes and relished the vibration of life that pulsed in her palm - the flutter of a barn swallow's wings and air rushing through its feathers as it darted through the rafters. Cool water rushing over the smooth rocks of the river, and the heavy drum of traffic beating across the warm asphalt blocks away.

The small salmon-colored stucco home sat at the end of D Street near the river's edge. A partition of elm trees filled the space between Isabella's house and Old Man Jackson's to the north. The house was colorful inside with rich hues of red, turquoise and yellow. Isabella's love of color overflowed from her mismatched wardrobe to the kaleidoscope of throw pillows on her couch. Monday she wore a Hawaiian print sundress, yellow flip-flops with silk fuchsia daisies over the strip between her toes, and pulled her shoulder-length hair back with a red and navy bandana.

People came from surrounding states to receive the miracle of Isabella's therapeutic massages. No one could explain it, but Isabella Martinez had magical hands. That's what everyone said, and the results of her work were undisputable.

By eleven-thirty, Isabella had worked on two clients, and was ready for her lunch break. She had everything ready to make a fresh Caesar salad with a side of fruit. Her next appointment was Frank at one o'clock. She looked at her watch, it was only noon, but Frank was always early. She washed down the last bites of her lunch with some lemon water, cleaned up the kitchen, and filled Samson, her Chihuahua's dish with fresh water. He took a drink and followed her back to work.

Frank, a tall, lean man with white hair, sat in the waiting area of her massage studio as she entered. The separate entrance her husband had built last summer came in very handy, especially with clients like Frank, who rarely knocked before he entered. Samson curled up on his purple and green paisley dog bed in the corner of the waiting area.

"Hi, Frank, how are you feeling today? How's the hip?" Isabella smiled down at Frank and motioned for him to follow her into the massage room.

Frank trailed behind her. "The hips been hurting again, can't lay on my right side at night."

The room was small with pictures of Jesus and the Madonna on the walls. A large philodendron occupied one corner and scented candles wafted through the room. A mobile of crystals hung from the corner opposite the plant, and a large crystal spear sat on the table under the shelf of lotions and oils.

"The blankets are on the foot of the table, go ahead and get undressed." As she made her way out, Isabella turned on a small cd player permeating the room with sounds of ocean waves slapping against the shore to the rhythm of flute music.

Three minutes later, Isabella tapped on the door. "Are you ready, Frank?"

"Yes." Her client called out from the other side.

Isabella flipped the doorknob hanger to *Do Not Disturb* as she entered the massage studio and began her work ritual. First, she laid warm damp towels over Frank's neck and feet. Then she chose the oils and lotions that called to her for his specific needs, and rubbed each of them between her palms to warm them before applying to his skin. She began with the sweet herbaceous scented Roman chamomile, calming both mind and body, followed by some Balsam Fir oil for his muscular aches and pains.

Isabella glided over Frank's tight muscles and joints, releasing his tension. For nearly ninety minutes, she kneaded and stroked with the ease of an eagle in flight, effortlessly soaring across turbulent air.

When Frank and Isabella came out of the massage room, Tina, a thirty-something lady, was sitting in the waiting area.

Isabella pointed to the small fridge sitting in the corner of the room. "Frank, don't forget your water. Remember, you have to flush out those toxins we just released."

Frank smiled and reached down to grab a bottle. "Thank you Isabella. My hip feels much better." He took a large swig of water and nodded at Tina as he left.

Tina had nearly fallen asleep listening to the gentle background music while waiting her turn. She stood up. "Are you ready for me?" she chirped.

"I need a few minutes to change the sheets and towels."

"No problem. I know I'm early, but figured waiting here a few minutes would be better than driving around."

Isabella retreated to the massage studio and washed her hands with the Agua de Flora, she used after every session. Cleansing was important between each person, releasing the residue of the previous client's troubles before touching the next was important. She replaced all the towels, blankets and the sheet on the bed, then went back out to the waiting room. She waved Tina in. Samson was still asleep in his bed.

Tina stripped down to her panties, climbed onto the table, then called out letting Isabella know she was ready. Tina pulled her waist-long hair off her back and over to one side.

Isabella prepared herself and gently smoothed the oils into Tina's tight and dry skin.

"Isa, when you touch me it's like the whole world melts away and I'm floating on a cloud."

Isabella smiled as she gently pushed the muscles outward from the spine. "Tina, you have a lot of heavy energy in your shoulder blades. It's very dense, especially over your right shoulder. What's going on?"

Tina winced. "We got a new manager at work, and he doesn't like me. He can't fire me, so I think he's trying to force me to quit. He's making my life miserable."

"I can pull the negative energy out, but I have to be careful not to absorb it myself, so I protect myself. It is the same out in the world. People give off energy and absorb energy. You need to protect yourself too."

"Protect myself? How can I do that?" Tina asked.

"I say a simple prayer for protection. But always be aware of who is around you, and what is going on. Haven't you ever heard of energy vampires? People who suck your energy. I understand they are common in many work places. Always protect yourself."

Isabella rubbed Tina's back and neck leaching the frustrations and fears out of her body with each movement across Tina's fair skin.

As the day went on, aroma therapy candles of ginger and spice pirouetted through the house on waves from the ceiling fan. After Tina was Sonya with a lower back pain, then the last client of the day was Larry, a truck driver who always came in before he went back out on the road.

After Larry left, and Isabella washed her hands for the last time, the phone rang. She lifted the handset of the yellow touchtone phone mounted on the kitchen wall. "Hola."

"Isabella, it's Cathy." Said the kind voice on the other end of the line.

"Hi Cathy, I was just thinking of you."

Samson romped into the room and looked up at Isabella with begging eyes. She tossed a dog biscuit down to him from the bowl on the counter.

Cathy hesitated on the other end of the line, then cleared her throat. "Aren't Ruth and Gabriella Santos a relation to you? I know it's been a long time, but I seem to remember them visiting you years ago. Or do I have the names confused with someone else?"

Isabella trembled as she reached for the bar stool and pulled it under her. She knew this call was a message of great sadness. "Yes, Ruth is my cousin, Gabriella is her daughter. I have not seen or heard from either of them in ten years. The last I heard they were down in Mexico somewhere. Why?"

Cathy let out an uncomfortable sigh. "Gabriella died, Isa. I'm so sorry."

Isabella's chin quivered and her eyes closed tight, but it did not stop the tears from falling.

Cathy continued. "I was packing my mother's things for her move, and had a stack of old newspapers to pack with. The date on the death notice was a month ago... The paper didn't say anything about family or a service. There's no obituary. I looked in other issues, but didn't see anything."

Tears cascaded down Isabella's smooth olive cheeks. She had expected to hear Ruth died, but not Gabriella, not the child.

Cathy's voice was soft. "I'm so sorry. Isa, please let me know if there's anything I can do."

Isabella placed the phone back in its cradle, and wept into her hands. She wiped her eyes, walked out and stood on the back porch where she listened to the birds, shedding the tears from her soul. When she was able to collect her thoughts, she strolled back into the kitchen, opened the drawer of the small desk next to the counter and pulled out the phone book. The corner of an old photograph under a pile of scattered notes and coupons, caught her eye. As she held the photo in her hand, snippets of the day flooded her memory. The three of them holding hands, perched on rocks at the river's edge, giggling as the cool water ran between their bare toes. Gabriella squealing as she chases the neighborhood tabby around the yard, just clever and quick enough to stay beyond the reach of the girl.

Gabriella ran to the porch and plunged into her mother's lap, panting, and asked for something to drink. Isabella brought out a pitcher of lemonade. Little Gabriella, sitting next to her mother, drinking cold lemonade and laughing.

Isabella took a picture with her Polaroid, gave it to Ruth, and took another for herself.

She was reminded of the conversation that reignited the arguments and the resentments. Ruth asked for money to go to Mexico to start over. She was making an effort to get clean, get off the drugs, and be a better mother. Ruth needed gas and food for the trip. She apologized for stealing, and asked Isabella to forgive her.

Isabella said nothing, but slipped a couple of twenty dollar bills into Ruth's hand. That was when little Gabriella plunged into her lap, looking up and asking, "Aunt Isa, do you forgive me?" mimicking her mother and giggling.

Isabella kissed the four-year old girl and whispered in her ear, "You are an angel, there is nothing to forgive." Her memory was not quite as faded as the old photo.

Isabella thumbed through her phone book until she found the number she looked for, then dialed.

"Hello, my name is Isabella Martinez. My cousin's death notice was in your paper last month, and I need some information. Yes, I'll hold." Sensing her pain, Samson paced around her feet until his ears perked up and he scampered off to the living room.

"Isa, I'm home." The front screen door slammed shut behind her husband, Leo, as he entered the house. He took his ball cap off and tossed it on the table as he strolled through the kitchen. He wrapped his arms around Isabella standing behind her, snuggling his chin into the curve of her neck.

Isabella pushed his hands off, stepped forward and raised a trembling finger to signal she needed a minute to finish the call. "Where are her ashes now?"

Leo stepped around to see her face wet from the tears. She scribbled some notes on a tablet as she listened to the person on the other end of the line.

"Thank you," Isabella said as she hung up the phone and fell forward into Leo's embrace and sobbed against his chest.

Leo held her tight in his arms until she pulled back and swiped her eyes and nose. He searched her ebony eyes.

"What is it, Isa?" Leo wiped a tear from her face.

"Gabriella's dead. They won't tell me anything except that she died as a ward of the state." Isabella's chin quivered with each syllable.

Leo draped his arms around her and held her tight.

"I have to find out what happened. Where is Ruth when all this is going on? And why didn't she tell me?"

Leo put his hands on Isabella's shoulders. The tall slender man looked down into her red and swollen eyes. "Sweetheart, you cut ties with Ruth long ago. She has no other family."

Isabella tightened her jaw. "But to let her daughter be raised in the system by foster families? That is not our way and she knew it. Gabriella would have been loved here. And now look, instead she is dead." She collapsed into her husband's arms, heaving sobs. Leo held her tight, rocked side to side and hummed.

Leo put a hand under Isabella's chin and gently lifted it up to bring her eyes to his. "Is there anything we can do? Have they had a service for her?"

Isabella shook her head sideways. "She was cremated. Her ashes are somewhere in the chaos of government processing bullshit."

"We will go get her ashes. We will make another shelf on your alter just for her."

Isabella let herself weep.

After dinner, Leo went out to his workshop behind the garage to cut a shelf. In the house, Isabelle stood in front of the altar, lit a candle, and prayed. Pictures of her mother and father sat to one side, and of her grandmother and Aunt Rosa, Ruth's mother, on the other side. In the middle of all the portraits stood a colorful statue of Madonna holding a newborn child in one arm, and a spray of white lilies in the other. She placed the Polaroid of Ruth and Gabriella next to Rosa's, and positioned two bowls in front of it, one bowl holding a lemon representing the bitterness of life, the other bowl holding candy for life's sweetness.

On Tuesday, Isabella cancelled all of her client appointments so she and Leo could make the hour long drive from Ontario to Caldwell to pick up the ashes of her cousin's daughter. The Mexican radio station played music that Isabella was in no mood for, but knew it would keep Leo entertained. So instead of voicing protests, she turned inside herself. Leo understood Isabella was in no mood to talk when she leaned her head against the window, so he hummed to Mariachi music as he drove.

Isabella marched into the coroner's office with identification in hand and determination in her step. "My name is Isabella Martinez, I understand you have the remains of my cousin, Gabriella Santos, and I'm here to pick them up."

The clerk behind the desk was an overweight, middle-aged woman with snarly grey hair. She nervously thumbed through a stack of paperwork and searched her computer. "Oh yes, here it is, Gabriella Santos, age 14. She was cremated August tenth. Do you have verification of guardianship over the remains?"

Leo put his hands on Isabella's shoulders to hold her down.

"Guardianship? I am her family! Her mother is my cousin." Isabella's voice escalated with each word in anger and frustration. "Where is her mother? She'll tell you."

"I'm sorry Mrs. Martinez, but without legal guardianship paperwork, I can't release the ashes; and according to my records, her mother is deceased as well, and there are no living relatives." Isabella stomped her foot on the floor. "I'm living! And I'm her relative."

The clerk shrugged her shoulders unable to help.

Isabella spun toward Leo, her dark brown eyes begged for help.

"Where do we get the authorization for guardianship of Gabriella's ashes?" Leo asked in a tone calculated to keep his wife calm and the clerk helpful.

"For a ward of the state, the main Department of Health and Welfare office on State Street, behind the capitol, in Boise."

It struck Leo as sad that the clerk knew the answer so readily. "We'll get it taken care of and be back. In the meantime, do you know where her belongings are?" Leo asked.

The clerk shook her head and let out a heavy sigh. "Nothing came to us. You might check at the children's counseling center over on 12th Street, where she was when she…" Her words trailed off in instant regret.

"Thank you." Leo said over his shoulder, as he pulled his wife out of the room.

Isabella, red with blood pumping to every capillary in her face, escaped her husband's grasp when they entered the hall. "I want Gabriella's ashes, and I want them now. I'm gonna' have me a long talk with Jesus when I get home tonight." She put her head down and plowed out of the building. Leo followed in her wake.

Isabella climbed in their Ford pickup and pulled her seatbelt across her chest snapping it in place. Leo gave her a questioning look. "Health and Welfare?"

She waved at the road ahead. "Yes, we'll get the paperwork then we'll stop by the counseling center on the way back."

Leo nodded compliantly and put the pickup in gear.

Isabella rummaged through her purse for some gum. "Our family has never been right. I look at your family and it's big and they're close. I never had a family, just one thieving drug addict cousin who would do anything to get her next fix. And now she's dead too?"

Leo turned on to State Street. "Yes, and you had put these emotions away a long time ago."

"But I never knew Gabriella needed a home."

"That's right, hon, you never knew, and you would have been a wonderful mother to her if you had been given the chance." Leo smiled reassuringly.

"It's not fair. It's not right and I've had this conversation with Jesus many times. Why I can't have children, but someone like Ruth can? It's not fair."

After acquiring the necessary paperwork and instructions, they left Boise and headed back for Caldwell.

Leo pulled into the small parking lot of the large stone building where a statue of playing children stood beneath the protective limbs of a large tree. Isabella's eyes fixed on the bronze boy and girl. Leo got out of the pickup, walked

FORGOTTEN LIVES: *Where Evil Lurks*

to the passenger side, took Isabella's hand and helped her out. They headed up the wide cement stairs leading to the double door entry. Leo opened the entrance for Isabella. She stood in the lobby, it was welcoming with comfortable chairs and books.

A young lady with spikey hair and double piercings in her ears sat behind the window of the reception desk. She smiled at Isabella. "Can I help you?"

Isabella wanted to smile back, but it just wasn't there. She pursed her lips instead. "I've come to get the personal belongings of my cousin, Gabriella Santos."

The receptionist's expression shifted. She turned, picked up the phone, and dialed a number, her words stammered. "Maya, there's someone down here for Gabriella's belongings. Uh huh, okay." She hung up the phone. "If you want to have a seat, our Director will be right with you."

Leo and Isabella looked around the room behind them, and retreated to a pair of chairs next to the fireplace. Leo picked up a magazine about parenting and thumbed through it. Isabella was too anxious to look at anything.

Within five minutes Maya Sanderson entered the room. She reached her hand out to Isabella and Leo. "Hi, I'm

90

Maya, the Director of the Treasure Valley Counseling center. You're Gabriella's cousin?"

Isabella stood up. "Her mother was my cousin. I haven't seen Gabriella since she was a toddler. I had no idea what was going on. If I had, this never would have happened. We take care of our own." Pain filled every syllable.

Maya smiled at her. "Please, won't you come to my office? It's just up one floor."

Leo and Isabella followed Maya up the stairs to her corner office on the second floor. They sat on the comfortable couch and Maya placed the cardboard box on the coffee table in front of them. "I'm so glad to meet you, and thankful you are here to collect her things."

Isabella looked at the box and trembled as she reached to touch it. "This is Gabriella's? Is this all she had?"

"I'm afraid it's all that came from her last foster home. Foster kids usually don't have much. Clothes are handed down and items are often lost or stolen. I understand her mother died in prison some years back. The records showed she had no other relatives."

"Ruth and I didn't always see eye to eye." Isabella's words were filled with spite. "She stole my money, my credit cards, but when she stole my wedding ring to hock for drugs..." Isabella's jaw tightened as she looked at Leo.

"Well, I threatened to turn her in to the police, but I never actually did it. She packed up what little she had and Gabriella, and said she was going to Mexico to find Gaby's father. I never heard from her again."

Isabella slowly opened the top of the box and looked inside. A tattered and faded teddy bear, a small jewelry box, a few pictures, a journal and a framed picture of Ruth. Isabella's hands trembled too much to investigate further. She closed the lid and pulled the box onto her lap. "Did you know Gabriella?"

Maya smiled. "I did know her, not as well as I would have liked. She was a very generous and caring young lady."

Isabella stared into Maya's eyes. Had they met before? She didn't remember, and yet, there was something very familiar. "You do a great service for the children here, don't you?"

"We certainly do all we can," Maya said. "Our counselors see on the average 90 children a day here. We work very hard to help them. I would love to put you on our mailing list for our newsletter. I plan on a special dedication at our next Gala for Gabriella. Maybe would like to come?"

Isabella's hands encircled the box on her lap. "I would like that. I'll bet Gabriella really liked it here. She liked you, didn't she?"

Maya nodded. "Yes, I think so, on both accounts."

Leo and Isabella stood up. Isabella took a business card out of her purse and gave it to Maya. "Here is my contact information. Put me on your mailing list, and let me know about your Gala." They shook hands and left.

Leo offered to carry the box out to the pickup, but Isabella tightened her grip more securely around it, not wanting to let go. The drive back to Ontario was quiet, with Isabella's mind on her cousins, and the stories the box on her lap might tell.

It was late afternoon and the school buses were dropping off the last of the children to their homes.

Leo turned down D Street and pulled into the garage. He turned the pickup off and looked over at Isabella. "You're awfully quiet, sweetheart. What's on your mind?"

Isabella looked down at the box. "Just thinking about Gabriella's life. When I saw the school bus, I wondered what schools she attended. Who were her friends? Was she a good student, and what subjects did she like the most?"

Leo gently laid his hand over Isabella's. "If I know you, honey, you will have these conversations with her. Just because she is no longer in her body, she can still talk to you. You've always had that gift."

Isabella tilted her head and looked at Leo, and her heart felt relieved for a moment, as the tightness in her chest relaxed. She loosened the grip on the box. He was right. She understood, more than most, the death of a body was not the end of a life. What was truly Gabriella, still existed. She nodded at her husband with the hint of a smile.

Isabella placed the box on the floor next to her altar in the small alcove off of the bedroom, and entered her office. She knew there would be emails and messages, as there was any time she took off work. After sifting through all the needs and concerns of others, Isabella retreated to the kitchen to make dinner.

As the food cooked, she lit a single white candle in the center of the round dining room table, then crushed some lavender and sprinkled it around the base of the candle. Finally, Isabella called into the living room where Leo was watching the news. "Dinner is ready, come join me."

Leo turned the television off and grabbed a beer out of the refrigerator, kissed Isabella on the forehead, and sat down at the table. "Honey, this smells wonderful." He piled the tossed green salad onto his plate, buttered two rolls, and took a large bite of the tender chicken. As he chewed his first bite, a smile of satisfaction spread across his face.

Isabella reached out and touched Leo's left hand as he ate. She had not taken a bite yet. "I know we sometimes get so busy with our lives, you with the construction work, me with my massage patients, but I want you to know how grateful I am for you. I realize now, more than ever, how lonely Ruth was. She had a baby who was more of an inconvenience to her than anything else."

Leo gave her a troubled look. "You know that Ruth loved her little girl. I know she had a lot of problems, and she was not the best parent, certainly not the way you would have been. But she did love her."

Isabella looked up to the ceiling searching for the right words. "I know she loved her. I don't mean to imply she didn't. Ruth was troubled her whole life. I know she suffered abuse her whole life. All I'm saying, is if she'd had someone in her life, the way I have you, I truly believe both she and Gaby would be alive today. And happy."

Leo took her hand and kissed the back of it. "You're probably right. But not everyone is as blessed as we are." He kissed her hand again, winked and dove into his dinner.

As the sun set in the evening sky and the kitchen was cleaned for another day, Leo settled in front of the television for an evening of sports. Isabella poured herself a glass of lemonade, meandered into her sitting room, and eased into the chaise beside her altar. She opened the box and extracted the journal that lay on the top. Her heart felt heavy with the precious book in her hands. "I need some fresh air." Isabella said to Samson, who sat at her feet, looking up at her. She held the journal to her chest and left the room.

"Honey, I'm going to be on the back porch if you need anything," Isabella said to Leo as she passed through the living room. He turned to smile and blow her a kiss.

Isabella wandered out the back door of the kitchen and onto the screened-in porch that spanned the width of the house. The floor was covered with an old braided rug her mother had made. Two wicker chairs with soft floral cushions sat in one corner, plants lined the outside wall and statues of angels and the Virgin Mary filled spaces in between. She sat, sipped her lemonade and opened the journal. She listened to the river flowing, and the birds singing in the weeping willow, then began to read.

In the beginning there were pages of poetry, and stories of friendships forged with her counselor and Mrs.

Sanderson. She spoke of proud moments showing off good grades and honors achieved at school. Then the positive entries became fewer and the words became dark with pain and turmoil. Each page weighed heavier on Isabella's heart.

Then rape!

Isabella dropped the book and gasped with shock. Catching her breath, she snatched the journal off the floor and ran into the living room. She stood between Leo and the television, holding the book open in her hands like a burning stone she could not handle. Leo turned the television off and stood to look at the page she offered. He read the words and closed the book, pulling Isabella to him.

"We cannot change the past. But we can pray for her soul to be released from all this pain now." They swayed in each other's arms in the middle of the living room.

Isabella started the following morning going through Gabriella's box. She had cancelled her appointments for the day, giving her time to devote to preparing Gabriella's altar. She sat on the floor next to the altar with Samson on her lap. She opened the box and pulled out one item at a time, reflecting on the energy of the item and feeling the troubled soul of a young girl.

Halfway through the box, she stood up and laid a hand crocheted doily, over the new shelf Leo added to the altar. She carefully arranged a glass Virgin Mary candle, a picture of Gabriella, a small rosary, a silver chain with a Saint George charm on it, and a dried rose pressed between two sheets of wax paper that were all in the box. In the jewelry case was Gabriella's silver baby ring on a delicate tiny chain which Isabella slipped over the edge of the picture frame. Gabriella looked so happy in the picture.

Isabella lit the Virgin Mary candle, then the two white candles on either side of it, sat down on the chaise and made the sign of the cross, touching her forehead, her heart, and each shoulder. She held her own rosary in her hands as she closed her eyes and prayed for the soul of her cousins.

As she sat in silent prayer, a sound startled Isabella, a jagged echo of a voice that frightened her.

"He is here for you, … Isa, don't let … in." The voice faded in and out, it was hard to understand.

"He?" Isabella asked, "he, who? Did someone do this to you, Gabriella?"

The voice lowered to a whisper. "He wants you."

A sudden chill swept through the room. The cold swiped Isabella's face and blew out the three candles. She stood up in defiance holding her rosary to her chest and her other hand out in a stopping motion. "You will not enter here, and you will release Gabriella!" she bellowed with all the strength she could muster.

The breeze vanished as quickly as it appeared. Samson shivered underneath a blanket at the foot of the chaise. Isabella gulped. She placed a small copal incense burner on Gabriella's shelf and lit it and the candles again. She sprinkled sea salt around the table for the continuance of life. She pulled marigolds from a basket and lined the edge of the table, then for added protection, pulled some apart and sprinkled petals around the base of the altar. She placed a white porcelain statue of the Virgin Mary next to Gabriella's photo, and filled in all the empty spots with marbles, some small crystals, and the hair clips from Gabriella's box. She wedged the worn teddy bear near the back of the altar. She sat back down, closed her eyes and prayed.

Samson barked. Isabella looked around to see if anyone was there. She was still alone. She looked at her watch, it was nearly four o'clock. *Where had the day gone?* She wondered. *I need to get to church.*

The Blessed Sacrament Catholic church was not far, and Isabella didn't want to miss the four o'clock confessions.

Her chest was constricted with burdens she needed to release. She was relieved to see the sanctuary nearly empty. She lit candles for the souls of Gabriella and Ruth, then slid into the confessional and touched her forehead, her heart, then left and right shoulders making the sign of a cross.

"In the name of the Father, and of the Son, and of the Holy Spirit, Amen." She took in a deep breath collecting her thoughts. "Bless me Father, for I have sinned. I am a forty-five year old wife with no children." Isabella paused. "It has been three months since my last confession, and these are my sins. I turned my cousin away years ago, when I should have helped her. I should have done more, but I was so angry with her, and judgmental, I could not see clearly. Now she and her daughter are both dead and I am filled with regret and anger against myself." She took a deep breath. "And a few times last month I lied to my husband and told him I had a headache when I didn't. I was just tired and didn't want to hurt his feelings. I am sorry for these sins, and the sins of my whole life. I ask for forgiveness, absolution, and penance."

The gentle voice from the other half of the confessional replied. "It is never easy to know the correct course of action when dealing with others, especially family. We must always pray to God the Father for guidance, and trust He knows best. Let go of the anger and regrets, and let the Father show you His love and healing powers of the spirit," the priest said. "Go make things right with your husband, and anyone else you need to. Then say ten Hail Mary's and three Our Father's. Go in peace."

Isabella bowed her head. "Thank you, Father." She left the cathedral with a lighter heart and a new hope. She would pray now for Gabriella's soul and focus on healing them both, as well as Ruth. She spent the rest of the week attending to only two clients a day, giving her extra hours to pray at Gabriella's altar. Each day she spent an hour in the morning and another in the afternoon, holding one of the items from Gabriella's altar with her eyes closed, imagining the girl that cherished the teddy bear, the necklace, and the journal. She recreated the years she had missed, in her mind, and ending each session seeing herself hug and kiss the girl.

Sunday was a welcome relief to Isabella. It was her holy day, no work, just worship and relaxation. After mass, she met her friend Cathy for lunch at Romio's Pizza and Pasta on South Oregon Street. They were both creatures of habit, never even taking the menu to consider something new. They knew what they liked and they stuck with it. To

Isabella, the baked fettuccini formaggi, was better than ice cream on a hot summer day.

Cathy was a pizza girl and always had Romio's special with pepperoni, Canadian bacon, mushrooms, black olives and Italian sausage.

Isabella washed down a bite of pasta with a sip of red wine. "How is your mother handling the move?" She asked her friend.

Cathy shook her head. "Not so well. She calls me daily to tell me what is wrong. Yesterday someone had stolen her quilt. Of course I found out later it was in the laundry. The day before that she thought someone had taken all her little candy treats she had hidden in her night stand. But they hadn't, she'd just forgotten she ate them." The two friends laughed.

Cathy's expression got serious, and she leaned forward. "How are you doing? I mean after finding out about Ruth and Gabriella? What exactly happened?"

Isabella knew Cathy was hesitant to ask. Details of personal family pains were not normally open for discussion. But Isabella needed to confide, and Cathy was the one friend she trusted. She set her fork down to give her thoughts full attention.

"The last time I saw them I hated Ruth. I was so angry at her for everything. I hated her drug addiction, her lifestyle, and her lying and cheating. But most of all I hated that she had a beautiful daughter and I couldn't have any." Isabella stopped to wipe tears from her eyes before they fell down her face. She took another deep breath and regained her composure. "Now I hate myself for letting her go."

Cathy reached out and held her hand.

On Sundays, Isabella always prepared an early dinner so they could be done in time for the seven o'clock Mass. She had flour tortillas hot on the griddle when Leo got home from a day of fishing with his buddy, Ed.

"Isa, your sportsman is home." Leo walked in smiling, inhaling the fragrance of her home cooking. He grabbed a cold beer out of the fridge and sat down at the table while she finished the meal.

"Did you catch some fish?" she asked him.

"I caught three and Ed caught two. You know how he is, so I let him take them all home to his family." Leo took a long drink from the beer. "And yours? Did you have a relaxing day?"

Isabella wiped her hands on her apron and brought a plate of tortillas to the table. Her face looked troubled. She sat down beside him, took the beer out of his hand, sipped a drink, and handed it back to him. "It was an unusual day. Over half of my customers have cancelled for this coming week. I've never had that happen before."

Isabella got up and went back over to the sink. She stared out the window draped in sheer yellow curtains. A clear blue sky greeted her view as she watched Old Man Jackson's grandchildren playing in the yard next door. She turned back around. "There was something else, something I'm not sure of."

Leo finished off the last of the beer and tossed the can in the recycle box next to the trash can. "What is it?"

Isabella brought the last of the food over to the table, took off her apron and sat down. "Let's eat. I'll feel better after we eat." She clasped her hands together and dropped her forehead on them, her eyes closed. In a moment she lifted her head, made the sign of the cross, and whispered, "Jesus, you know what to do." She looked up at her husband who was staring at her with a questioning look.

"It's been a very difficult week." She told him.

"How, Isa? What's going on now?"

Isabella looked at her plate. "I had a visitor the other day when I was setting up Gabriella's altar."

Leo looked confused. "Why didn't you tell me?" He stuffed a forkful of food in his mouth.

Isabella looked at him and sighed. "I needed time to process all of this and try to make sense of it. But I can't. I was visited by a very dark spirit. I believe it was connected to Gabriella's suicide."

Leo took another large bite and spoke as he chewed - something Isabella didn't like. "Go on, I'm listening."

"There is a dark force, not just one spirit, but a legion of spirits, of evil, that is at work here. I'm not sure yet what they had to do with Gabriella, but there was some connection."

Leo scraped the last of the food off of his plate. "And this legion came by here?"

Isabella was irritated. "Of course not. If a whole legion of evil came to this house, do you think it would still be standing?" She stood up agitated, unable to eat her dinner. She paced around the kitchen wringing her hands.

Leo pulled a second helping onto his plate. "My dear, Lucifer himself could not tear down this house with you in it. Of that I am certain. You have a host of angels at your back, and there is nothing stronger."

Isabella thought for a moment about this statement. Her husband was right. This dark shadow which crept into her space might have frightened her, but she had a much stronger power at her disposal. She had Jesus at her side.

She felt better. She sat back down at the table and nibbled at her dinner. She placed her hand over Leo's and smiled. "Thank you for believing in me."

Leo leaned over and kissed her. She could smell the chili peppers and cilantro on his breath. "My darling, your strength is the life force of this home. As long as I have you, I know I have nothing to ever worry about." He picked up his plate and took it to the sink. "You and my nine millimeter, that is," he said with a laugh.

Isabella slowly chewed the small bite of food in her mouth. She wanted to believe him - that there was nothing to fear, but no gun in this world could stop the evil she had felt. How did it get so close to her? And how could she make sure it never came back?

Isabella cleaned up the kitchen and loaded the dishwasher, while Leo showered and changed for evening mass.

The phone was ringing when they arrived home after the Sunday evening mass, and Isabella hurried into the kitchen to answer it. "Hola."

It was silent for a moment, but as she started to say hello again, a slow and deliberate voice came on the other end. "My name is Manuel. I am nearly paralyzed from an infection that raged through my body for over a month.

The doctors have finally cleared it all up, but I have hardly no range of motion in my legs and arms. I was told you were the person who could help me. This is Isabella, right?" he asked.

Isabella was silent now. Another voice, not in the room or on the phone, was speaking to her as well. "Hang up now," the unseen talker said. "Hang up now."

"Hello, are you still there? I was referred to you by my doctor, he said you could help me," Manuel said.

Isabella felt sick to her stomach, but she never turned away someone in need of help. "Of course," she said, "I can see you tomorrow. Can you get to my home?"

"Yes, thank you." His voice sounded relieved. "My doctor said you live at the end of D street east, near the river?"

"That's right," Isabella said. "We're the last place before the river. I can see you first thing in the morning, say nine?"

"Thank you," Manuel replied. "I will be there at nine."

Isabella hung up the phone and headed over to the couch, but halfway there she doubled over with a severe cramp in her stomach.

Leo jumped out of his chair to help her. Before she could call his name, his arms were around her, guiding her to the couch and easing her onto the soft cushions.

"What is it? Are you okay?" Leo asked.

Isabella shook her head. "I don't know."

Leo sat down and held his wife, brushing the hair out of her face. "Should I take you to the hospital?" he asked.

Isabella sniffled and shook her head. "No, it's nothing like that. I'll be okay." She scooted down and laid her head in Leo's lap not wanting either of them to move.

The morning sun poked through the gap between the two heavy red curtains covering their bedroom windows. Leo was in the shower. Isabella rolled over and rubbed her eyes. She was stiff and needed to stretch. She sat up on the side of the bed and arched her back, reaching her hands toward the ceiling. She glanced down at the clock and realized she better get breakfast started. She pulled her soft turquoise robe off the hook on the back of the bedroom door, slid her feet into her fuzzy pink slippers and yawned as she made her way to the kitchen.

The chickens in the coop out back were clucking and the rooster crowed his morning greeting.

"Good morning to you too." Isabella said as she started the coffee pot. She twisted left then right, trying to get the night's heavy sleep out of her body.

As the coffee brewed, Isabella stepped onto the back porch and rubbed her fingers over her rosary beads as she said her morning greetings to all of nature. Samson followed her, always one step behind. She heard a faint whisper behind her. Not sure if it was just the breeze rustling in the tree branches, or someone actually in her yard, she turned with the rosary to her chest. Isabella gasped when she saw the transparent figure of a young beautiful girl standing in the corner of the porch. Gabriella held her hand out, pointing in the direction of the river. Her voice was soft, but Isabella heard it clearly. "He comes for you, beware."

The image faded but a whisper lingered in the morning breeze. "In the water, you can save her."

Isabella stood frozen, her rosary clasped to her heart. She finally took a breath when she heard Leo in the kitchen. She blinked a few times and ran into the house.

Leo poured his cup of coffee. "Isa, what in the heck is wrong?"

Isabella held the rosary tight in her fingers looking back and forth expecting someone to enter the room. "I saw her. I saw Gabriella. And she was telling me something."

Leo leaned back against the counter and sipped his black coffee. "What was she telling you?"

Isabella shook her head. "I don't know. Beware, that's what she said."

"That doesn't give you much to go on, does it? Beware of what?" Leo asked.

Isabella bit her lower lip. "I don't know, I gotta' have me a talk with Jesus, I need more direction than this." She wrung her hands as she headed toward the bathroom. The door closed behind her and the shower started. She would cleanse, she would pray, and then she would listen.

When Isabella came out of the bathroom, Leo was already gone to work. After she released her wet hair from the towel wrapped around her head, and slipped on a bright orange and white striped dress and green flip flops, Isabella lit incense in every corner of the house, and candles in every room. Then she lit the four candles on the two shelves of her altar, knelt down with her rosary beads in her hands, and lowered her head. "Help me Jesus, help Gabriella speak to me clearly so I may understand this message. Speak to me now." She cleared her mind of all thoughts, with only the vision of the burning Virgin Mary candle in her mind, and waited. Her knees began to hurt from kneeling on the floor, so without opening her eyes, she changed to a lotus sitting position, and continued to listen. She rubbed her fingers over the prayer beads of her rosary, one by one, asking for clarity.

In the darkness of Isabella's mind, she saw the single flame of the candle burning brightly. Then something moved behind the flame and she saw a man's large hand clasped to the wrist of someone much smaller, much younger. The frail arm struggled to get free of the grip, but it was useless. The large hand overpowered her, and held her down.

Isabella tried to see more, but the vision disappeared. She took a deep breath expanding her lungs, relaxing her shoulders, listening. She could hear the water of the river rushing, the sound of someone hiking through the pebbles along the shore. She heard a clock chime ten times and a dog bark in the distance. She could hear a person gasping for air, and a gurgling sound of someone under water. And then everything went black and silent. No flame, no sound, only the void beyond the veil of life and death.

Isabella opened her eyes. She shivered, even though the temperature was nearly eighty degrees already. She looked at her watch. It was eight thirty. She shuddered from the grief of the vision that had just left her. Such pain and sorrow. She shuffled into the kitchen and poured herself a cup of coffee and filled her dog's dish with fresh water. Samson lapped it up immediately.

"There you go, Samson. We must keep hydrated in this hot time of year." Isabella looked at her coffee cup and smiled.

Isabella watched the shiny black car of Manuel, her new client pull into the driveway. She had an odd feeling as he opened his car door. Her stomach began to cramp again, but not as severely as the night before. This was not a good sign. She remembered she had not done her protection prayer this morning, but there was no time now. She greeted him at the front door. Samson barked furiously. Isabella held the small dog to try and keep him quiet.

Isabella's hand rested on the front door, holding it open as Manuel entered. A friction burned through the wood of the door into her palm like a raging fire. She quickly jerked her palm away and rubbed it.

"Something wrong?" Manuel looked up at her and raised his eyebrows.

Isabella's hand trembled slightly. She had never felt this impression before. "No, just a strange sensation, nothing to worry about." And yet, it did worry her.

Manuel stepped inside the house. His back hunched over, he heaved a deep breath. His eyes were dull and sunken under bushy eyebrows. He looked at Isabella. "Thank you again for seeing me on such short notice. My doctor said you might be hard to get into, but worth the effort." He flinched with pain as he moved in slow motion.

"It's alright, follow me." Isabella led him into her massage room. Samson was still at his heels yapping. Isabella put the small dog in her bedroom and closed the door. The massage room was filled with burning candles and incense burned in all four corners of the room. She pointed to the massage table. "Go ahead and disrobe to your level of comfort, then lay face down on the table. You can place the blankets at the foot of the table over your body, and when you're ready I'll come back in and get started." She hit the play button on the CD player, but nothing happened. She opened it up and it looked fine. She tried again, but it wouldn't play.

"I guess we won't have any music today," Isabella said.

Manuel grunted as he struggled to get his shirt off. "It's okay. I don't need it."

"Is there anything I can help you with?" Isabella asked.

Manuel shook his head sideways. "No, I'm fine."

She left the room with one hand over her stomach. Maybe she was coming down with the flu or something. She felt very uneasy.

In five minutes Isabella tapped on the door and Manuel signaled he was ready for her to come in. She washed her hands, then poured some peppermint oil in one palm, and rubbed her hands together to warm it up. She spread the oil into his shoulder blades and down the center of his back. She kneaded his tight muscles from the spine outward, then up around the neck. All of his energy was so heavy and dark, like nothing she had ever encountered before.

Normally, when Isabella worked on a client, she felt the dense energy lift from their body. But Manuel's energy was impenetrable, and it pulled her into him, which felt prickly and stung her hands. Isabella tried to release her hands from his skin, but they wouldn't pull away. Her palms and fingers became one with Manuel's back. His pain and stiffness transferred through pulses of energy into her body. Her vision began to dim and blur, as if she were entering a dark tunnel. She gasped for breath. The pain was paralyzing her.

Isabella's hands released and she fell to the floor, unable to move. Her eyes looked up at Manuel as he stood up, erect and limber. She couldn't move her lips or speak. She wanted to shout at him, to stop whatever he was doing to her. Her hands were numb. She was completely disconnected from her body, from the universe.

What evil was this that had trapped her spirit?

Manuel leered at her, grabbed her wrists and pulled her up. She was totally paralyzed, unable to struggle or scream. He dragged her out the back door and down to the river's edge.

Manuel flung Isabella's body into the river. She floated for a moment, then slowly sank. Manuel stumbled into the water behind her and pushed her body under the surface. His movements were slow, taunting her, relishing the panic in her eyes. She was helpless. She watched the cold water rush over her face and threaten to take her life. The water stung her eyes.

Isabella's thoughts raced through her mind. *What happened?* If only she could get her hands to move. His evil face sneered at her from above the water's surface. Panic began to be replaced with peace. Her life was leaving her body. The water was no longer cold and dark, but comforting. She couldn't move and so she gave in as the air left her lungs. The angels would take her now. She floated with the current of the river as Manuel kept a hand on her chest, holding her down.

A white light flashed above the water and suddenly Isabella could move her feet. It was difficult at first, but there was some control. She concentrated with her last ounce of life to push her feet into the riverbed. Her limbs felt as though they weighed a hundred pounds each. Movement returned to her arm, and gradually, before death took control, she managed to force one arm up as she rolled her body out from under Manuel, and pushed his hand off of her. She pushed her head above water, sputtering and gasped for air. Every breath brought her another ounce of energy, and a faster movement in her step as she wedged her feet more firmly into the rocks on the river bottom. She put everything she had into getting more control.

Manuel grabbed her and pushed her all the way under the water, his strong hands around her throat. Isabella held her breath and kicked his legs causing him to fall in the river, allowing her to break free again.

She swam to the edge of the water. Before Isabella could reach the bank, he grabbed her ankles and pulled her back. His strength was ten times greater than hers, but she had a force within her he didn't count on. She surfaced again with a gasp and reached for the bank a second time. Water splashed as they fought. She heard a loud crack and Manuel released his grip and fell into the water, sinking under the current.

Isabella burst through the surface. She gasped for air and coughed up water, shuddering from the cold river. She looked around trying to understand what happened. Old Man Jackson was standing in the water with a baseball bat. He grinned, exposing a half-toothless smile. He reached out to grab her hand and help her to the shore.

In the distance the old mantle clock in the living room chimed ten, and Samson barked from the bedroom window. Isabella smiled.

A young girl peered out from behind the large tree at the water's edge. Old Man Jackson wrapped his arm around Isabella as she shivered. He handed the bat to the girl and motioned for her to follow them as he escorted Isabella up to her house.

"How did you know to come?" Isabella asked Old Man Jackson.

"My granddaughter, Gabby, saw you and ran to tell me to grab the bat and follow her, she said you were being dragged to the river." He looked over at the girl and winked.

Isabella stepped over and hugged the girl. "You are an angel." She turned to look at the river, watching for Manuel to come up from the water for air, but he had disappeared with the current.

Gabriella looked up at Isabella. "I don't like the man with red eyes. He scared me." She looked to the river.

Isabella collapsed in the grass and sobbed. All her fears came in at once and piled down on top of her, crushing her spirit, tormenting her mind. Old Man Jackson helped her up to her feet and escorted her back to her porch.

"You'll be fine now, Isabella. He's gone."

Isabella wanted to believe him. She nodded in agreement and waved at them as they left. But she wasn't convinced. She locked the door on her back porch and sat in one of the wicker chairs after lighting all the candles for protection. She curled up in a ball and wrapped her arms around her knees as she drew them into her chest. *What if this happens again?* She thought. *What if someone else comes, or he comes back? What if there's no one to save me next time?* She dropped her head and wept.

That evening Leo came home to find Isabella still sitting on the back porch, staring mindlessly into the trees that lined the back of their property.

"Sweetheart, what's wrong?" Leo could see trouble in her distant eyes.

Isabella shook her head and explained the evil man who used her gift against her and tried to kill her. Leo fell to his knees and caressed her.

"I could never live without you. God will not let anyone take you away from me." He stood up and took her hand, pulling her up. "Come on, I'll take you out to dinner."

The restaurant was nice, the food was good, but Isabella was speechless. She was still so distraught over the day's events, she couldn't pull herself back. Leo put his hand on hers.

"Honey, why don't you take a few days off. Maybe visit your friend, Patricia, in Jackpot. Spend some fun time and take your mind off of the normal. Take a break."

Isabella looked up at Leo and smiled briefly. "I am going to take a break. I'm not going to see any clients for a while. Not until I can forget this. Maybe never."

Leo raised his eyebrows. "Never? But honey, you have such a gift, and you heal so many people."

Isabella shook her head again. "A gift that can be used against me is not much of a gift. Perhaps I need to find something else to do. I don't want to talk about it anymore." She took another small bite of food.

Leo nodded in understanding. She needed time to heal.

Isabella spent the rest of the week emailing everyone she knew, and calling the rest to let them know she was taking a hiatus from her massage work. She would let them know when she could see clients again. But she was nauseous every time she thought about touching someone, rubbing her hands across their skin, being pulled in and rendered helpless and vulnerable. She didn't know if she would ever be able to go back.

The color had gone out of Isabella's life. She wore jeans and Leo's black tee shirts, no shoes and nothing in her hair. For weeks she spoke to no one. She read books and magazines, watched old black and white movies on television and played with her dog, Samson. She couldn't even walk past the door to her massage studio, and considered tearing the wall out beside it and turning it into something else.

Early one morning after Leo left for work, Isabella found herself on the back porch, lighting the candles and the incense, resting her hand on the corner post to feel the dance of life again. She had been afraid to touch anything since the day Manuel had come. But she forced herself that day. She closed her eyes and sensed the birds soaring through the sky above, gliding on the gentle current of air that held them between the flaps of their wings. And just as she began to pull her hand back, a voice whispered in her ear.

"Is this your choice?"

Isabella opened her eyes wide and looked around, but there was no one there. She whispered back. "What do you mean?"

The voice elaborated. "Is this your choice? To live in fear, to give up your power? Is this your choice?"

Isabella felt the pounding of her heart as if it would burst out of her chest. She had been gripped with fear, and she didn't know how to move beyond it. She tightened her fists and marched into the house with Samson close behind. She strode up to the door of her massage room and reached down to take hold of the knob. Just a half an inch away she stopped. She couldn't do it.

Samson followed Isabella as she turned on her heels and marched into her bedroom. She opened a small jewelry box and pulled out her special Rosary Novena. She held it tight in her hands and closed her eyes. "I will pray the

Novena, and at the end, I will be ready to open that door. Saint Ann will give me strength." She winked at Samson.

For nine days and nine nights, Isabella stepped up to her massage room door with her Rosary in hand, prayed, and turned away. She spent the time in her sitting room, sipping lemonade and making her special prayers at Gabriella's altar.

On the tenth day Isabella stood in front of the massage door again. Samson stood beside her. She gulped. It was time.

"What if..." Isabella looked down at Samson and he barked back up at her. She took in a huge breath and swiftly grabbed the door knob and opened it. The room was the same as she had last left it. Dusty, but the same. She quickly lit all the candles and said a prayer as she paced around the room and around the massage table. She couldn't stop. She said the prayer over and over, pacing continuously around the table. She collapsed on the table, flooded with visions of all the people she had helped. Frank, Sonya, Tina, and the hundreds of clients she had seen over the years. She saw their smiles, their warm embraces of gratitude, and sensed the joy of healing that was her gift to give. She wept in the knowledge that God had entrusted her with a special power, a connection to the

Oneness of spirit, and she could not forsake that. She prayed to Jesus to forgive her. A soft voice spoke in her ear.

"You are an angel, there is nothing to forgive."

That evening after dinner, Isabella and Leo sat on the back porch, drinking a glass of red wine and relaxing in the glow of the sunset. She slipped her flip flops off and rested her bare feet on a small foot stool. Samson jumped up and snuggled in a ball on her lap.

Leo smiled at his beautiful wife. "I trust you had a good day? I see you are wearing your colorful clothes again."

Isabella returned his smile, looking down at the blue and pink polka-dotted dress. "Yes. I broke through it." She took a drink of wine.

Leo scratched his head. "You broke through what, dear?" He placed his hand over hers and squeezed.

"I broke through my fear today. I went in the room and released my fears to Jesus." Leo raised an eyebrow and beamed. "You're going to start working again?"

"Yes. I sent out messages to everyone. I'm going to start on Monday."

Leo held out his glass of wine to hers to clink them together in a congratulatory toast.

A storm was coming, but not one a meteorologist could forecast. Isabella felt it in the tingle in her fingers, and an itching of her palms. Change was coming on the heels of thunder and lightning, and it would bring with it a battle. She had to let go of the fear if she was going to win this fight.

She would don her armor.

RAYE

The Communicator

Tumbleweeds marched through the empty desert in ranks of unstoppable force. From southern Idaho they swarmed over the border into northern Nevada with no acknowledgment of boundaries. A squad of prickly branches rolled across the lonely highway in Jackpot, Nevada and halted against the front steps of a single wide trailer in the small park a block and a half east of the casino.

The rented trailers were inhabited by employees of four casinos, two hotels and a convenience store that formed the nexus of the small secluded community of Jackpot, or what Raye referred to as middle earth. She had come here on a weekend getaway two years earlier, after her divorce, and took a job without giving it much thought, except that it would be a place to help her heal.

Raye opened the door of her trailer home and pushed the tumbleweeds aside. She glanced up into the afternoon

October sky and rubbed the tiger eye necklace draped around her neck. Her window sills were lined with blue crystal gem stones for spiritual protection from this ominous time.

Friday the 13th, and a full moon.

Inside, Raye lit three large white candles on the small counter between the living room and kitchen. Incense burned in each corner of the living room. Jinx, her black cat rested on the back of the couch as Raye chanted.

> *"I call upon the ancient powers;*
> *To help me in this darkest hour."*

Raye swallowed a drink of water and continued.

> *"Guardian Angel, bring your light;*
> *Make my future days be bright;*
> *Embrace me with protective wings;*
> *Guard me from all harmful things.*
> *I ask this for both Jinx and me.*
> *As I will – so mote it be."*

Raye could already sense the full moon high up in the grey Nevada sky, even though it wasn't yet visible. She brushed her jet black hair, freshened up her red lipstick, and blew out the candles. She looked at the black cat staring up at her. "It's time for me to go to work, you guard the house and I'll be home later." She petted him, locked the door of her home, and marched the block and a half to the rear entrance of the six story casino. She worked the afternoon shift in the Pair o' Dice Styling Salon.

The styling salon held two stations split between Kathy and Heather on the morning shift, and Chloe and Raye on the afternoon shift. Raye didn't mind following Kathy, who was a neat freak ensuring the chair and counter were always spotless when Raye took over at two o'clock.

Chloe was in her twenties, a skinny girl with a purple stripe of hair in her otherwise blond curls, a nose and eyebrow piercing, and nails which were always painted black. Raye was a bit more conservative at the age of 53. Although she did have a tattoo of a ruby red slipper on her right shoulder blade to remind her that she always had the power to get what she wanted. Her biggest trouble was knowing what she wanted.

Raye was wiping down the counter and the chair, when her four o'clock appointment came in looking nervous. The woman was in her mid-thirties with mousy brown hair pulled back in a ponytail, and dark circles under her eyes suggesting she'd not slept in days. She gazed downward as she spoke.

127

"I have an appointment," she mumbled. "My name's Linda."

Raye smiled, though the woman didn't look up to notice. "Go ahead and have a seat Linda, what is it I can do for you today?"

"I want a change. I want to look like someone else. Can you do that?" Linda said in a hesitant meek voice.

Raye wrapped a small white cloth around her neck, then draped the large black plastic apron across Linda's chest, snapping it at the back of her neck. "Sure, who do you want to look like?" She chuckled.

Linda's face contorted in agony, eyes closed tight, teeth gritted. It was painful for her to even think about a transformation. She slowly relaxed, opened her eyes, and bit her lower lip. "Just different. I don't want to look like me anymore."

Raye brushed through Linda's hair. "Okay, we can cut it short, and color it? Give you a cute style that says, 'Hey look at me, I'm sassy'. What do you think?"

Linda flinched. "I don't want people to notice me. The cut and color's fine, but nothing that's going to stand out. Okay?"

Raye understood. Her voice softened. "It's okay, I get it. You want to hide. We can do that too," she said. Raye led

128

Linda to the chair in front of the sink and gently pulled her hair under the warm water.

As Raye combed, dyed, cut and styled, she tried to carry on a conversation, as she always did with customers. But every question she asked was returned only with silence, so Raye talked about herself, her cat Jinx, and the band playing in the Gala room that night. When she was done, Linda looked completely different. The transformation was complete from shoulder-length strait mousy brown hair, Linda now sported short strawberry blond hair.

"Mission accomplished," Raye said as she handed Linda a mirror to check it out for herself.

"It looks good," Linda said as she smiled for the first time. She paid Raye with cash, then reached under her blouse, and removed a necklace of ruby red stones surrounded by glittering diamonds. Raye wasn't certain they were genuine, but they sparkled as if they were. Linda laid the necklace on the counter. "This is for you, a gift."

Chloe was folding towels at her station since she didn't have a client. Her mouth dropped at the stunning piece of jewelry and moved closer to examine it. "This looks real!" She said.

Raye turned back around. "Ma'am, I can't take this," she said, but Linda had already left. Raye darted out into the casino, but Linda had vanished into the crowd of weekend gamblers. She went back in the salon and looked at Chloe. "I don't know what to do with it. Do you really think it's genuine? Why would she give it away?"

Chloe shrugged as she put the last of the folded towels in the cupboards.

"Put it on," Chloe said. "That's a heck of a tip!"

Raye picked up the necklace then dropped it just as quickly, pulling her fingers to her mouth. "Ouch. It cut me!" She stared at the brilliant red stones and got a Band-Aid out of the cupboard to put over the end of her finger. Her stomach cramped causing her to bend forward. She decided to scoop the necklace into her tote bag and examine it later.

"I don't know, I've never had anything with diamonds before," Raye said.

"Not even a wedding ring?" Chloe asked.

Raye smirked. "I was married once. We had matching gold bands, no diamonds."

Chloe put a hand on her hip and grinned. "I never knew you were married. What happened?"

"Life, I suppose." Raye waved her hand in the air. "There's really not much to tell. He was a jerk and he broke my heart."

"Do you have any kids?" Chloe asked.

"No, I have Jinx. Now can we stop with the twenty questions?" Raye said.

"Okay. I'll bet you still love him, don't you? I don't get over past relationships well, either," Chloe said.

Raye gave her a warning look with one eyebrow raised. "Dirty towels in the hamper."

Chloe complied and put all the dirty towels away, finished sweeping the floor and made sure everything was turned off. She put on her jacket and winked at Raye as she headed out the door. "Good night."

Raye wiped her counter down, put all the bottles away and set the trash out to be emptied. She dropped her gaze to the tote bag and the mysterious ruby necklace inside. She hesitated picking it up, then scoffed at herself for being so superstitious. *It's just a necklace*, she thought, and yet her hand hesitated as she reached for the tote bag. She put her coat on and grabbed the tote bag in one swift motion, and headed out the door.

It was seven o'clock and the salon was closed for the night. Raye locked the door and took the back exit to head home. Her stomach was feeling more nauseous with every step. She felt an uncomfortable ache in her arm that cradled the bag. As she strolled the block and a half home, she glanced up at the full moon, now clearly visible in the early evening sky.

The full moon was when all the crazies came out to play, and in Jackpot, Nevada, that was just about everyone.

Crystals and wind chimes hung from the edge of Raye's patio roof, and greeted her with their music as she arrived home.

Raye dropped her tote bag at the end of the couch, pulled off her work clothes and slipped on a comfortable pair of sweat pants, and an oversized tee. She fixed a grilled cheese sandwich, and poured a glass of milk. She hoped it would settle her stomach. She fed Jinx the last of the milk and a stale burrito from the fridge.

She stood in front of the refrigerator for a moment, longing for the love that had once existed in the old picture stuck to the door with a magnet. The picture was taken on their tenth anniversary, Keith with his arms wrapped around her at a dinner, laughing at some stupid joke a friend had made. She loved his laugh, his embrace, and his stupid friends. For twenty-three years she loved him. But who was she kidding, she still loved him. Divorce didn't change her heart, only her marital status on her W-2's.

After dinner, Raye snuggled into her favorite chair with a light throw blanket across her lap and read a new Nora

Roberts novel. At the end of every chapter, her attention shifted to the bag at the end of the couch. But even looking at it made her stomach growl. Her eyes returned to the page.

Outside the sky was pitch dark in the desert at night. No city lights. Nothing but sagebrush, jackrabbits, and coyotes filled the empty space for hundreds of miles in all directions. The only exceptions were the lights from the four casinos and the full moon that hung high overhead.

Jinx meowed next to the door. Raye marked her spot, set the book down, and went outside with her cat. Jinx preferred the driveway gravel to a litter box. Raye admired the small string of colored lights draped over the lip of the awning, while she waited for the cat.

Going back in, Raye locked the door behind them. As she brushed past the tote bag, she sensed a sharp cutting pain, and jerked her leg up. She sat on the bar stool rubbing her calf until the pain was gone, her eyes fixed on the tote bag and its mysterious contents.

"Enough," Raye said to Jinx who was sitting at her feet. "Time for bed." The black cat looked up and meowed. Raye glanced down at the tote bag with an uneasy feeling. "I'm not sure what to do with you yet. I guess I'll sleep on it." She turned the light off and headed to the bedroom.

Covered in her cotton sheets, Raye saw a strange cloud form in the corner of her small bedroom. It slowly took shape as two bony hands that reached out to strangle her. Wrapped around her throat, pushing, the hands began to bleed.

Pain!

Can't breathe!

Raye coughed and woke up from the frightening dream, brushing the sweat from her brow. She rubbed her neck and shuffled into the tiny bathroom. She swallowed a drink of cool water and looked into the mirror; there was a smear of blood on her throat! Returning to bed, she tossed and turned the rest of the night with visions of being strangled and blood dripping from her blankets.

On Saturday, Raye got ready for work. She filled Jinx's dish and cut an apple to take with her. She pulled a smaller tote bag out of the pantry, not wanting to deal with the necklace yet. She only had one appointment in the salon – Louise, a regular from town who always insisted Raye, and no one else, trim and style her hair. She decided to head up to the casino early for the weekend brunch. It was her way of treating herself after a hard week's work, especially considering she was a terrible cook.

Raye slowed her pace when she saw an ambulance, police cars, and a huge crowd gathered near the north entrance of the casino, then quickened her step to find out what was going on. Her friend, Patricia, who worked in housekeeping, sat just inside the door crying. A policeman hovered over her. Raye rushed to Patricia's side and knelt down, looking up into her friend's eyes.

"What is it, Patricia? What's happened?"

The policeman looked impatient, shifting his weight from side to side. "I'd like to know the same thing."

Patricia wiped her eyes and nose with a tissue. "I told you everything I know. I want to go home now." She said in her strong Mexican accent. The officer huffed his frustration and pushed through the crowd.

Raye helped Patricia to her feet, wrapped an arm around her, and nudged her to the door. "Come on, I'll walk you home."

Gawkers crowded around the entry making it difficult to push through. They pointed to the ambulance as the hotel security pushed them back out of the way. Finally Raye and Patricia escaped and hiked back to the trailer court.

"What was all that crazy about?" Raye asked.

Patricia wiped her nose again and pulled in a deep breath. "It was terrible. I opened 413 and a girl was curled up in a puddle of blood on the floor, just barely holding on to life, and her little sister, a two-year old, stabbed dead in the bathroom." She sobbed and stopped to regain her strength.

"Dead? In our hotel? Where's the parents?"

Patricia started walking again. "I heard them say the girls checked in with their mother yesterday morning. But she's nowhere to be found. Her vehicle's gone. The girl they're taking to the hospital doesn't look more than ten years old. But she was unconscious when I walked in. I don't think she's been able to tell them anything yet."

"The mother's name wasn't Linda, was it?" Raye asked.

Patricia shook her head at Raye and nodded. "I don't know. But you might ask Betty, she usually knows what's going on."

Raye tightened her arm around Patricia. "What a terrible thing for you to witness. How could someone commit such a horrific crime?"

Patricia shrugged her shoulders and mumbled something in Spanish making the sign of the cross over herself. "Why would a mother leave her daughters? You don't think her mother did it, do you?" Patricia sniffled.

Raye let out a heavy sigh. "I have no idea. But then I never figured out why my mother abandoned me, either."

Patricia looked at Raye with surprise. "What do you mean?"

Raye shrugged her shoulders. "Oh it's nothing really. I was orphaned at a very young age. I really don't remember much, I think it's just too painful, so I wiped it from my thoughts. I lived in an orphanage in Caldwell for nearly two years before being adopted. I used to think the orphanage was a castle and dragons patrolled the outside."

Patricia looked surprised. "I didn't know you lived in an orphanage. I didn't think there were any orphanages anymore."

"Oh, it's a children's counseling center now. I think the orphanage was actually closed in the late 70's."

"How terrible to live in such a place with no family."

"It wasn't all bad. I had friends there and we had secret hiding places we would sneak into. I would tell myself I was a lost princess in my big castle." She smiled. "Come on, we're just about to your place." Raye waited while Patricia unlocked her door and safely enter her trailer.

"Thank you, Raye. You are such a good friend," Patricia said over her shoulder as she crossed the threshold. She looked sad and tired as she closed the door. Raye paused for a moment before returning to the casino.

When Raye arrived, she hoped to talk to Betty, the concierge, but the perky red head was busy helping two pot-bellied, fifty-something men who were obviously appreciating the benefits of the young woman's impeccable posture. She made her way through the slot machine rows to the café for her morning coffee, to give Betty time to help the men. She waited a moment, then headed to the information desk where she could be an excuse for Betty to terminate the advances that inevitably followed her assistance.

When the men turned away, Betty mouthed "Thank you," while she slid a laminated map of Jackpot under the desk, then reassumed her "May I help you?" position as Raye stepped up to the counter. "Hi Raye!" she said, with a smile middle-age flirts never saw.

"Hey Betty, I had a customer in the salon yesterday. She was a thirtyish gal about five foot five, brown shoulder length hair. I think her name is Linda, but I don't know her last name. Do you happen to know anything about her? She left a necklace in the salon and I want to get it back to her."

"Lots of ladies come through here, was she with anyone?"

Raye pursed her lips. "I think she checked in with two little girls."

Betty's eyes grew big and her voice lowered. "If I know who you're talking about, she checked in as Linda Shaner from Kuna, and paid for the room with cash, in advance - but they found out today that wasn't her real name. What's more, security said the address she gave was for a farm that was sold and turned into a business complex five years ago."

"Linda Shaner, huh? Do they have anything on her husband, where's he?" Raye asked.

Raye leaned in close. "Wiley told me her husband's in prison. So the two girls Patricia found, were in Linda's room?"

Betty nodded her confirmation, and Raye's hands folded over her stomach, in reply. Bad news always made her gut queasy.

"What do I do with her necklace?"

Betty shrugged. "You could always turn it in to the lost and found."

Raye was lost in thought as she absently waved goodbye to Betty and meandered through the crowd of weekend gamblers on her way to the salon. She wished she had been able to get Linda, or whatever her real name was, to talk to her.

The afternoon proved to be busy with three walk-ins. It was hard for Raye to concentrate as she shampooed a client's hair. She was haunted all day by visions of two helpless girls and a mother she'd helped transform. *And why did she need to change?* Raye wondered as she trimmed a young woman's hair. Did the mother do this to her own children, and Raye helped her to escape by changing her appearance? Guilt riddled her thoughts with every brush of hair. She glanced over at Chloe who was shampooing an older lady.

"I think I need to talk to the police," Raye said.

The young lady in Raye's chair jerked in surprise.

Chloe shook her head and continued shampooing. "You're over reacting. You did your job and she gave you a tip in the form of jewelry. It doesn't mean anything more than that. You always over-think things."

"But what if…" Raye frowned not even wanting to say the words.

"For Christ's sake, Raye, it's not like you're a plastic surgeon or anything. She's still recognizable. All you did was change her hair, not her face or her body."

The lady in Raye's chair fidgeted nervously. Raye didn't pay attention.

"I thought she might have been wanting to get away from a bad relationship, you know, maybe running from some abusive jerk."

Chloe rinsed her client's hair. "Maybe that's it. Maybe there was a man involved, he caught up with her, and attacked the girls and kidnapped the mother. The police will figure it all out. You worry too much."

Raye handed the young lady in her chair a mirror to look at the back of her hair. "How does it look?"

The blond nodded. "Looks great, thanks." She wrote a check as fast as she could and rushed out of the salon.

Chloe's older client didn't seem bothered by the conversation. Chloe towel dried her hair and combed it out.

Raye wiped her chair down and swept the cut hair off the floor. "I don't know, I still feel uneasy about this. It's got my stomach tied up in knots."

Raye passed Betty's desk on her way out, and Betty waved her over.

"Did you hear?" Betty asked.

"What?" Raye leaned in close.

"The girl they took to the hospital died in transit. And still no sign of the mother."

Raye's heart sank and her stomach swirled in turmoil. She shook her head. "I will never understand it."

Betty nodded. "I know what you mean."

It was nearly six o'clock by the time Raye got home, and Jinx was waiting for her at the door, meowing his story for the day. Raye petted him and lit her white candles around the living room, for clearing and protection.

"Really? You don't say." Raye would say in replay. She loved carrying on conversations with her big black cat, and Jinx was quite the talker. "Well I'll tell you what, there was a murder in the hotel. So terribly sad. And now the sister is dead too. What evil is this? And I may have been instrumental in some way by changing their mother. I'm so torn over this." She looked at Jinx as if the cat had the answer. He meowed back.

"Hmm. Funny thing is, it brought up old memories of my childhood. I wonder sometimes why things like this happen to children. Why does it happen to anyone?" She shrugged her shoulders and poured a glass of lemonade from the refrigerator. She looked down at the cat. "You want anything?" Jinx meowed again.

Raye shook a bag of kitty treats making Jinx twirl in a frenzy. She poured a small amount onto the kitchen floor and the shiny black cat gobbled them up.

"My mom used to always tell me whatever happened in life was a result of choices we make. So what fricken choice did these people make to kill two little girls? I just don't get it. Maybe it's not something that can be got!" Raye shook her head in disbelief and sat down on the couch with her glass and picked up her spell book – a large handmade journal that was created by her adoptive mother. Raye had added more spells to the book in the years she had it. The cover was hand-tooled cordovan leather, worn and faded with stains from spills over time.

Raye grabbed her tote bag and dumped the contents onto the coffee table. The ruby necklace slid out with a pack of gum, a dirty soup cup and a hairbrush. She was hesitant to touch the necklace again, it had a strange energy to it she didn't understand. She leaned back and stared at the necklace for a few minutes, but the longer she looked at its brilliant stones, the more her stomach churned in agony. She had to put it back in the bag and get it out of her sight. She reached her hand toward the piece of jewelry, but just as her fingertips neared it, the necklace flew off the table and onto the floor. Raye's eyes enlarged with shock, and a chill ran down her spine. Jinx hissed and jumped up on the back of the couch. Raye reached over to a small box on the end table, and fumbled around until she pulled out her pendulum.

"Does this necklace have something to do with the death of those little girls?" she asked but the pendulum hung motionless.

"Is this necklace stolen?" she asked. Jinx meowed and snuggled beside Raye on the couch. The pendulum still did not move. Raye clasped her hand over her mouth. She looked over at Jinx. "Oh my gosh, this has never happened!"

Jinx meowed. "Holy shit! I not only can't touch it, I'm not even to know anything about it. It doesn't make sense."

Jinx meowed again. "You're right. I'll turn it in to the lost and found. After all, I already told Betty it was left in there. That's what I'll do. Simple enough."

Raye bent down to shove the necklace back in the tote bag, but an unseen pressure pushed her back and she sat on the floor with her back pinned to the edge of the sofa. She understood one thing, she was not to have anything to do with the necklace. Her heart raced with fear. The tips of her fingers tingled with a strange energy.

Raye picked up her pendulum again. "Am I to turn the necklace into the lost and found?" The pendulum was completely still. Raye was confused. She tried one more time, held the pendulum higher, closed her eyes, and spoke slowly. "Is the necklace cursed?" she asked it. The pendulum did not move. She looked over at Jinx, who was rubbing her nose over a mouse-shaped catnip toy. "What's the deal? My pendulum always works."

The cat didn't know, or didn't care.

Raye leaned forward and held the pendulum closer to the necklace. Suddenly it was ripped from her hands and flew across the room, landing in a sprawling aloe vera plant at the end of the kitchen counter. Raye gasped, jumped up on the couch and backed into the corner, eyes wide with fear. "What the hell's going on here?"

Jinx jumped on the couch beside Raye, locked her gaze on the chain of the pendulum than dangled over the edge of the aloe. The cat arched her spine with her body poofed and her tail twitching. She hissed at the space between her and the plant.

Raye slowly moved her right hand in the direction of the necklace and stopped about two feet from it. "There's like a force field here. I can't touch it. Why would a necklace have a force field around it?" She looked over at Jinx, but the cat was too busy to answer. She got up and snatched the book of spells from the coffee table with one hand, Jinx with the other and flew out of the trailer.

Raye ran to Patricia's trailer and banged on the door. She didn't know which pounding was louder, her hand on the door or her heart in her chest. She looked over her shoulder, plagued by a feeling of being followed.

Patricia opened the door cautiously, peering through the small space.

"Pat, thank God you're home." Raye panted in fear looking back over her shoulder again.

Patricia pulled the door open ushering her friend inside, and shut the door quickly behind her.

"Raye! What's wrong? What's happened?" Patricia asked.

Raye stood with her back to the door, Jinx clutched under one arm, and the book under the other, trying to catch her breath and decide what to say.

Patricia shuffled to the kitchen, where she turned Cantina-loud Mariachi music blasting through a tinny radio on the window sill to a soft vibrant chant. "Come in, Amiga! Sit down." she said, waving her friend in as she passed by the entryway.

Raye followed her into the living room, where Pat turned off the muted TV.

"Bad magic Pat. Bad magic in my place - right now."

Raye stumbled and slumped into the recliner consuming a whole corner of the room. Jinx wiggled her way loose and jumped onto the window ledge.

Patricia sat down on the couch. "What do you mean, bad magic?"

Raye shook her head. "I think it has to do with the two girls you found." She wrapped her arms around herself, her eyes darting out the window in fear, her senses heightened, and the hair on the back of her neck was prickly.

"I knew it. I could feel something evil in the room." Patricia made the sign of the cross over her forehead, heart, and shoulders. "All I can see are those two little girls covered in blood. I can't get it out of my head. I can't eat or sleep."

"I know, Pat. It's been haunting me too like something is after me, but I don't know quite what. Then, this lady came in the salon Friday afternoon and wanted a complete makeover for her hair. You know, a different cut, color, the whole works. She wanted to look completely different."

Patricia nodded in understanding.

Raye continued, "she didn't want to stand out, she wanted to blend in. So I took care of her."

"You are so good with hair," Patricia said as she nervously rubbed her rosary beads.

"The lady paid in cash when she was done and left a beautiful ruby necklace as a tip."

Patricia smiled. "A ruby necklace? I get excited when I get a twenty for a tip. What did she say about it?"

"Well that's the thing. She didn't really talk at all. I tried everything just to strike up a casual conversation, but she was tight-lipped. By the time I realized the value of the necklace, she was long gone," Raye said.

Thomas, Patricia's thirteen year old son came out of the bedroom. "Mama, can I go to Randy's now?"

Patricia frowned at him. "Did you get all your chores done?"

"Si, dinner dishes are put away and my bedroom is clean." He bounced in anticipation.

Patricia looked over to Raye and whispered, "Is it safe?"

Raye shrugged her shoulders. "I don't know what's safe right now."

"Not tonight. You can have him come over here, but I don't want you going out right now."

Thomas opened his mouth to protest, but seeing his mother's warning stare, he slumped his shoulders instead and shuffled back to his bedroom.

"So how does this tie into the girls?" Patricia turned back to Raye looking puzzled.

"She was their mother."

Patricia gasped, clutching her hand over her mouth, she got up and paced the room.

"What's more, I talked with Betty who found out the lady checked in under a false name with a bogus address and info," Raye added.

"So what makes you think there's bad magic?"

"The necklace! When I touched it, it pricked my finger and made it bleed. I slid it out of my tote bag tonight and it flew away from me. It even caused my pendulum to fly out of my hand and across the room."

Patricia's eyes were stricken with fear as she stumbled backwards until she was in the corner.

Jinx meowed at something outside the window.

"I think the necklace is cursed," Raye replied. "I don't know how or why, but I get a sense of darkness and pain. Something evil is connected to it." She sat back and sucked in a large breath of air as if it was an asthma inhaler.

Patricia grabbed her rosary and crossed her forehead, heart and shoulders. "Oh we must pray to Jesus for protection."

Raye patted the leather covered journal on her lap. "Prayers, and I have my spells for protection." She rubbed her tiger eye necklace. "I have to find out who the necklace belongs to, though."

Patricia looked puzzled. "How are you going to find out who the true owner is? The people staying in that room weren't exactly the precious gemstone sort. They still haven't found the mother, and has anyone heard from the father? Who can you ask about it?"

"I don't know yet. This is an old necklace. If my sensors are right, it's close to a hundred years old, and I'll bet neither the mother or the father, whoever he is, would have answers."

Patricia sat down on the couch. "Then the true owner is probably dead."

Raye looked at her and laughed. "My friend, you are so right. Why didn't I think of that? I need to do a séance!"

Patricia got up and nervously paced the room again. "No, no. You cannot invite spirits into my home. I am sorry, but you will have to find someplace else to do that."

Raye smiled and looked over at Jinx sitting in the window ledge. "It's okay, Pat, I understand, and I think I know where I can do it."

Patricia's phone rang and she answered it. "Hola."

As Patricia chattered in Spanish, Raye flipped through the oldest section of her spell book looking for the pages of séance instructions.

"Okay, Amiga, see you Wednesday." Patricia ended the call and turned back to Raye smiling. "That was my good friend Isabella Martinez. She is coming down from Oregon for a visit next week."

"Oh, she's the massage genius you're always raving about, right?"

"Yes, you will be amazed when Isa touches you."

"I hope you'll bring her over for drinks on the patio so I can meet her," Raye replied. "We've talked about her so much, I feel like I already know her." She stood up, tucked the oversized book under one arm, and grabbed Jinx with the other. "Thanks again for everything. I'll head over to see if Leah's home. She loves this kind of stuff."

Patricia walked her to the door. "You let me know if you need anything. Just don't bring any bad spirits with you, okay?" She still had her rosary tight in one hand, and gave Raye a big hug in the doorway.

"No worries, I'll talk to you tomorrow." Raye turned and she and Jinx headed left to Leah's doublewide at the back corner of the small trailer court.

As the day turned to night, the temperature in the desert dropped and Raye quickened her pace to Leah's. Jinx meowed wanting down.

"We're almost there," Raye assured her cat.

Leah, a large-busted woman with an inviting smile and an infectious laugh, was unloading groceries from her car when Raye reached her place.

"Well hello neighbor, taking the cat for a walk? And I see you're doing some light reading?" She chuckled as she pointed to the huge book under Raye's arm.

"Something like that. Jinx and I need a place to stay tonight. I was hoping your couch had a vacancy for the night?"

Leah opened the front door. "My house is always open to you. But I haven't had the pleasure of Jinx staying here before. I don't have a litter box, will that be a problem?"

Raye walked in the homey living room decorated in an African motif with painted death masks hanging on the walls. She set the cat down on the floor. "No, he's actually trained to go outside."

Leah set her purse and a shopping bag on the kitchen counter and started putting the groceries away. "So what's up?"

Raye looked around. "Don't think I'm crazy, but I have a spirit in my place and I can't stay there until I get it out."

Leah shrugged and smiled. "What's crazy about that?"

"I knew you'd understand."

Leah held out a beer. "You want a cold one?"

Raye let out a sigh, relaxed her shoulders and took the bottle. "Thanks, I could really use this right now."

Leah opened a bottle for herself and sat down on the couch. "So whose spirit is overstaying their welcome?"

Raye sat in an overstuffed chair and rested her feet on the ottoman. Jinx jumped up in her lap and curled into a ball. "I suspect some bitch who wants her necklace back."

Leah raised an eyebrow with intrigue. "Do tell me more."

"I was given a ruby necklace by a client. But apparently, the necklace is cursed, or haunted, or something."

"Where's the necklace now?"

"Still in my trailer."

Leah furrowed her brow as she took a drink of beer.

"What is it, Leah?" Raye asked.

"This morning at work, a man came asking about you. He wanted to know your work schedule and where you lived. Just because I work at the information desk, doesn't mean I'll give out that kind of info. So, of course I didn't tell him anything, just pleaded stupidity," Leah laughed. "I'm good at that."

"What man?"

Leah took a deep breath. "I call him chain man. He had one of those huge chains hooked to his belt with the other end stuffed into his pocket. I'm sure the size of those links were compensating for something," She chuckled. "Anyway, chain man was about forty, looked like he'd been traveling a while. But I didn't think he wanted his hair styled, if you know what I mean?"

"Did you get his name?" Raye asked.

"No, chain man didn't give a name or anything else.

Raye took a drink of beer. "He didn't say anything, huh?"

"No…" Leah started, then her eyes lit up. "Yes! He said you styled his wife's hair, or something like that." She shrugged and sat back. "Do you think the necklace is stolen?"

"I tried to find something out about it with my pendulum, but the necklace and my pendulum both went flying across the room. So I don't know anything about it."

"They flew across the room? Awesome! So what now?" Leah asked.

Raye opened her spell book. "I'm hoping there's a spirit connected to the necklace who can answer that for us."

Leah smiled. "Séance?"

"You read my mind," Raye nodded. "You got white candles? We need white ones. The more the better." She finished her beer, got up and set the empty bottle on the kitchen counter. "We need at least one more person. Can't have less than three."

Leah leaned forward and got up. "I have some candles in the closet, I'll go see what's in there." She headed for the bedroom. "What about McLean? He's always up for a touch of the occult."

"Who's McLean?" Raye asked.

"He's the new bartender across the street. Moved here a couple of months ago, but a really nice guy. I'll call him and see what he's up to." Leah stopped at the kitchen counter, grabbed her cell phone, found McLean in her contacts, and pushed the call icon to dial. "McLean? Hey, this is Leah. I have a friend over here at my place and we want to do a séance, but need a third. You interested?" She looked at Raye and winked as she listened to his response. "As soon as you can get here…Thanks McLean, you're a sweetheart."

"Yes," Leah said, as she pressed the screen to disconnect. "He gets off work in an hour, and said he'll come straight over," she continued as she set her phone on the counter between the kitchen and living room. "Said he'd bring something for the festivities too. That man knows how to make a hell of a good drink." Leah smacked her lips.

"Okay! In the meantime we can get ready," Raye said as she marked the page in her spell book.

Leah headed into the bedroom and returned with an armful of candles and holders. "Here we are," She said as she placed them all on the dining room table. "Three tapers, two brass holders and one silver. And a slew of tea light candles."

The two women cleared everything off of Leah's small round table and scooted it to the center of the room. Raye pushed the three white taper candles into the holders, lit them, and placed them in the center of the table, and created a larger circle around them with the tea light candles. Leah placed a plate of grapes next to the candles, and a small basket of cookies.

"Too bad we don't have the necklace," Leah said. "We could put it in the center of the table to draw your spirit to the conversation."

Raye placed the spell book on the table, opened to the conjuring page, then stopped for a moment. "You're right, we really do need it. I'll be right back," She said, as she snatched her sweater from the back of a chair.

As she headed home, Raye pulled the heavy sweater tight to shield herself from the chilly wind that seemed to be getting stronger. She stopped at the corner of the trailer next to hers. Lights were on and someone was in her trailer, a person stooping and moving like he was searching for something. *Is he looking for the necklace?*

Raye crouched down and ran to the end of her trailer, where she could peek in through the living room window without the threat of being exposed by a street light. She couldn't get a clear view.

Raye stood still and looked up at the brilliant stars that filled the night sky. Trouble was near, she could feel it. Her stomach churned.

Heavy footsteps scooted through the gravel behind her. Raye froze. She held her breath, her mind and heart raced. *Oh shit!*

The man in black jeans and a black hooded sweatshirt seemed more of a shadow than a person in the moon light. Raye wasn't sure if she was seeing his face, or her idea of it, in the recess of the hood pulled taut and forward on his head. She gulped. "Who are you? What do you want?"

The stranger sized her up and down. "You the stylist from the salon?" he asked, with the scratchy voice of a heavy smoker.

"Who wants to know?" Raye asked, nervously. She glanced down at the large chain that hung from his belt.

"Don't mess with me bitch. I want to know where my girlfriend is, now!" He stepped closer to her with each word. Raye's breathing sped faster with each step.

"I have to find her. You fixed her hair, didn't you?" He dropped his hood back and ran his fingers through his thick dark hair. He was agitated and his hands trembled. "Did she leave anything behind? Some jewelry?"

Raye stood motionless for a moment. "You're not after your girlfriend, you're after the necklace."

Chain man grabbed her shoulders and shook her. "Do you know where it is?" he screamed in desperation. He let go of her and turned around, then turned back around to face her again. "I have to find the necklace, it's death. That necklace is death."

"You mean finding the necklace is a matter of life and death?" Raye asked.

"No lady, I mean that necklace is death itself." He fidgeted and nervously looked back and forth. "Just give me the necklace, lady, please." His voice was filled with the desperation of a drug addict begging for a fix.

Raye stepped back. She nodded her head in understanding. "Your girlfriend's daughters had the necklace, didn't they?"

Chain man's chin quivered. "I have to get the necklace back. Do you know where it is or not?"

"It was in my living room. I was just coming to get it."

Chain man peered at Raye. "It's not in there now. I already searched."

Raye fiddled with the keys in her hand. "Let's look again, together."

They walked around to the front door, chain man opened the door for her. "My name's Clint." He followed Raye into the narrow living room.

Raye looked up at him, watching his every move. "I'm Raye. Where did you get the necklace?" Raye stepped over to the aloe vera plant and picked up her pendulum first and slid it into her pocket. She looked on the floor where she had last seen the necklace, but Clint was right, it wasn't there.

"I stole it. I...I didn't know the damn thing was cursed."

"What do you mean, cursed?" Raye shuffled through magazines and papers on the counter hoping to find the necklace.

Clint rubbed his stubbly chin. "Apparently, it was this old lady's necklace, and she wanted to wear it to her grave. And then someone stole it off her, right out of the casket."

"Wait a minute," Raye said as she held up a hand in a stopping motion. "You stole a necklace off a corpse in a casket?"

Clint whimpered running his hand through his hair nervously. "My buddy, Aaron was the one who took it off her. I mean, she was dead and all. They were going to bury this piece that's worth a lot of money!"

Raye sat down on a bar stool and stared at him dumbfounded. "Go on, I can't wait to hear the rest."

"Look, I don't have a lot of time, lady, I need to get the necklace back."

Raye looked around the room and shook her head. "It's not here. I don't know where it is. But tell me why you think the necklace is cursed."

Clint turned around, then back around again, unable to decide what to do. "Aaron's wife was in the car, so she put it on first."

Raye narrowed her eyes on him. "When was this?"

Clint looked up and mumbled, calculating the time frame. "It's been two weeks. And in two weeks, everyone who has put that necklace on has died. Everyone!" He paced the small area in front of the door. "Aaron's wife, Aaron, the waitress at the coffee shop." He clinched his fist and hit the door.

"Your girlfriend had the necklace on when she came in my shop. Is she dead, Clint?"

Clint continued to run his fingers through his hair and swerved back and forth in a panic. "I don't know, I think so." His eyes were red trying to hold back tears.

"I think the woman you stole the necklace off, wants it back. Do you know who she was?" Raye asked.

"I think Lisa said her name was Olivia, or something like that. I don't know. I was going to pawn it, but then Lisa found it and fell in love with it. Her littlest girl wore it first, playing dress up. In fact I think both her daughters took turns wearing it."

"Lisa's your girlfriend? She told me her name was Linda."

"Linda's her twin sister."

Raye held her hand up in a stopping motion again. "Let me see if I can find it. Hold on." She held up the pendulum and asked, "Is Olivia's ruby necklace here?" She stood motionless waiting for the pendulum to swing, but nothing happened. She asked again, "is the ruby necklace here?" The pendulum swung forcefully side to side.

"What does that mean?" Clint asked.

"It means the necklace is gone. Did you see anyone around when you got here?"

Clint shook his head. "No, but your front door was open, like a few inches. I didn't break in. Honest."

Raye smirked, "even though you are a thief. And you had every intention of breaking in, didn't you?"

Clint let out a sigh. "I knocked first and called out to see if anyone was home. My girlfriend's daughters are dead, and I don't know where Lisa is. I'm desperate, lady."

"I can see that." Raye looked at the door remembering when she left the trailer. She was sure she slammed it so it locked. She held the pendulum out again. "Did someone break in here and steal the ruby necklace?" The pendulum swung forward and back. She looked up at Clint. "Someone else has it."

Clint rocked his head down. "Ah shit, now what are we going to do?"

Raye stuffed her pendulum in her pocket. "Come on, we're going to find it." Raye motioned for Clint to follow her and led him to Leah's trailer.

When the pair stepped into Leah's, McLean was standing behind the kitchen counter mixing drinks. He held up a tumbler filled with ice and an amber liquid. "Drink anyone?"

Raye reached over and took the glass. "Don't mind if I do." She took a sip and made a sour face. "What is this?"

McLean smiled and held out his hand to shake Raye's. "It's an Old Fashioned. Good, isn't it? One of my favorites. I'm McLean, nice to meet you."

Raye gestured for Clint, still standing by the door, to come in. "Clint this is McLean, and Leah. Clint is Linda's, I mean Lisa's boyfriend. He's also the guy who originally stole the necklace off a dead corpse."

Leah gasped with shock. "Ew! You stole off a corpse?"

McLean held up his glass. "Wicked." He took a drink.

Clint backed up a little. "No, now wait just a minute there. I was not the one who stole it off the corpse. I'm the one who stole it from the guy who stole it from the corpse. I never saw the body."

Leah reached out to McLean. "I think I need a drink now. Make it a big one."

McLean finished his drink and poured two more. "I'm with you babe."

"I didn't know we were stealing from a corpse, not at first. Aaron had this plan and it sounded great, up until we got to the funeral home," Clint protested.

"Aaron wore the necklace?" Raye asked, taking another sip of her drink.

Clint paced around the room. "Well, it wasn't like he wanted to wear some old lady's necklace." Regret suddenly fit him like a fine tailored suit. "Okay, so I did know we were going to a funeral home. Those places are gold mines. And we figured it's not really stealing from a real person - the dead aren't going to miss anything." He looked at the stunned faces staring at him. "You should see some of the stuff that gets buried with these rich stiffs. It's crazy, a total waste!"

McLean took a drink. "Well you have my curiosity piqued. Although I'm not sure why."

Leah hit McLean on the shoulder. "That's just sick, sick and wrong."

Raye sat down at the round table in the middle of the room and motioned for the others to join her. "Okay, it's séance time. Come on. Obviously Clint has learned a valuable lesson here."

Clint sat beside Raye and turned to her with eyebrows raised. "What lesson?"

Raye frowned. "That some dead bodies *do* miss their possessions. Don't steal from the dead!"

Clint nodded. "Oh yeah, yeah, right."

McLean sat down at the table with a drink in hand. Leah turned off the overhead light so the room was lit only by candlelight. She sat down and took McLean's hand on one side, and Raye's on the other. The others followed and waited.

Raye closed her eyes. "Dearest Olivia, rightful owner of the beautiful ruby necklace which has been taken from you."

Clint squeezed her hand, and she squeezed it back even harder. "Commune with us Olivia, let us know if you are here."

They sat in silence. "Olivia," Raye called out again, "we want to return your necklace to you, but you must help us find it."

Again, they sat in silence, waiting for the ghostly response.

Leah's head fell back, then leveled and she spoke in a low gravely sound. "Not Olivia."

Raye's stomach did a triple spin and a somersault. "Who are you?"

The low voice continued, "Sarah Rhinehart."

"When did you have the necklace, Sarah?" Raye asked.

"Nineteen hundred and twenty-three."

"Was it stolen from you?"

"Yes. I want my necklace."

"How can we get the necklace back to you, Sarah?"

"Ashes to ashes, dust to dust."

Raye rolled her eyes not sure what that meant. "Where is the necklace now?" she asked.

"The boy, with black hair and black eyes."

Raye opened her eyes to look at Leah. "Patricia's son, Thomas?"

Leah's eyes were closed. "Stop the pain. Return the necklace."

"Thank you Sarah. Go in peace. We promise to return what is rightfully yours," Raye said and looked around the candlelit room. She noticed McLean open his eyes for just a moment, then close them again. Her stomach jumped into her chest at the sight, surely she was wrong. *Maybe it was just a reflection off the candle's flame.*

Leah's head tilted to her left shoulder and she opened her eyes and looked around the room at everyone. "What?"

"Some old ghost was talking through you," Clint stammered.

Leah looked at Raye and smiled. "For real? I channeled her? How cool is that?"

"Way cool!" said McLean. "Do it again!"

"Yes my friend, you did," Raye said as she rose from the table. "Okay, blow out all the candles. She peered at McLean again, and gulped in apprehension.

Leah held up her empty glass. "But I need a drink; my throat feels like the Sahara desert right now."

"Clint and I are going over to Pat's, hopefully she hasn't put the necklace on." Raye grabbed Clint's arm and pulled him out of the door with her.

It was dark and cold outside. But the night was well lit by the bright casino just a couple of blocks away. There was still a light on in Pat's trailer. Raye knocked on the door. She looked in the window but couldn't see anything. She pounded harder on the door.

"Patricia! Are you in there? Patricia!" Finally the door inched open and Thomas looked up at Raye with guilty eyes.

"I came over to borrow some milk and I saw it on the floor, I didn't mean to take it," he whined as Raye and Clint pushed their way into the trailer.

Raye ran up to Patricia, who was standing in front of a mirror in the living room holding the necklace up in front of her.

"Pat, don't put it on. Stop right there!" Raye moved steady to not startle her friend. Pat turned around and looked at her.

"Is this the necklace you got? This is the evil spirits?" Pat flung the necklace toward the door and Clint caught it before it hit the floor.

Raye scowled at Thomas. "Your mother would have died if she'd put that on!" He looked down at the floor in shame and scooted into the kitchen.

Clint's whole body convulsed and he dropped the necklace. He grabbed a dish towel off the counter and wrapped it around the necklace and picked it up. "What do I do with it now?"

Raye glared up at him. "You go put the damn thing back where it belongs, because I guarantee if you don't, Sarah will hunt you down and kill you, whether you put it on or not."

Clint shook his head and backed up to the door. "But I could sell this for a lot of money." His eyes were transfixed by the brilliant red stones, and his breathing became rapid with an adrenaline rush. His eyes lusted at the necklace in his hands. "I'll bet I could get over a hundred thousand for this."

"You moron! You can't spend a dime from the grave," Raye yelled.

Patricia grabbed her rosary off the table by a statue of Mary, and clutched it to her chest. "I couldn't breathe when I held the necklace up. It was so beautiful, but it made me suffocate just to hold it." She closed her eyes and mumbled a prayer with her face raised to the heavens.

Clint smiled, his eyes in a trance on the hypnotic stones that peered out of the folds of the towel. He stepped out of the door and looked back at Raye. "Thanks for finding this for me. It's my ticket out of here." He jumped off the step and ran into the darkness.

Raye's mouth gaped open. "What an idiot!" She shook her head. "What an absolute fricken idiot!" She walked over and hugged Patricia. "I'm so glad you're safe, I was so worried."

"I kept hearing a ringing in my ears when I picked up the necklace, like an echoing voice, that kept telling me 'don't put it on, it's here for Raye'. You were the one it came for, but you have a powerful guardian angel, my friend."

Raye smiled, "yes I do!"

Monday morning Raye sat in the cafeteria at the casino, nibbling on a blueberry pancake while she perused through her laptop.

Leah sat down in the booth with Raye. "Did you hear?" Leah asked as she stirred some sweetener in her coffee.

Raye sipped her coffee with French Vanilla creamer. "Hear what?"

"That guy Clint, they found him dead in a one vehicle rollover early this morning."

Raye huffed. "No! Did they find the necklace?"

Leah shook her head. "I don't know. Not only that, the mother was found halfway to Elko, run off the road, also dead. What are you working on?"

Raye gazed at the laptop. "Researching Sarah Rinehart."

"What did you find?" Leah leaned forward.

Raye swirled the last bite of her pancake in syrup and slid it into her mouth. She turned her laptop around for Leah to see it. "Sarah Claypool born in 1906, married Leonard Rinehart in 1923, died in 1991, survived by her only sister, Olivia Claypool."

Leah scrolled through the article. "So Olivia stole the necklace from her older sister and was going to be buried with it."

"Until two idiots came along," Raye smirked.

A week later Leah joined Raye on her small patio, the tiny lights around her awning twinkled like bright little stars. Jinx rubbed back and forth across their legs, then chased a bug at the edge of the grass.

They drank hot buttered rums that warmed them from the inside out. Raye watched the vast abyss above the desert and pointed to a shooting star.

"I still think about the necklace. I can't shake the events around such a beautiful, and yet, deadly piece of jewelry," Raye said. "And how I wasn't even able to hold it, maybe Pat's right, maybe my guardian angel has been putting in overtime with me." She laughed and took a drink of the hot rum.

Leah pulled a blanket over her lap and snuggled into the lawn chair. "Do you really think we have guardian angels?"

Raye took another sip of the warm drink and looked higher into the night sky. "I do. I could feel their presence when I lived in the orphanage, when I was just a little kid. I don't know how to explain it, I just always knew there was an angel watching over me."

Leah savored the tasty rum from her glass. "I don't believe in angels. It seems kind of weird to me. But I do believe in spirits."

"I've always believed there was something in my life that was waiting just beyond the veil of mortal vision. I don't know what it is, but I have a feeling someday I'll find out," Raye said. "It makes me wonder what I will find when all the planets align and the stars smile down from the heavens. What does God have in store for me?"

"Damn, girlfriend, either you've been drinking too much or I haven't had enough," Leah laughed.

"Maybe so. The necklace was only the beginning though. I've been having dreams, feelings of sorts, that it was only the tip of the proverbial iceberg. There's a storm brewing beyond the heavens, a storm of evil is coming." Raye searched the sparkling diamonds in the sky above.

"Maybe it's time to move out of the desert?" Leah asked.

"This storm is coming for me, it won't matter where I am. I keep seeing death and suffering."

"You've seen your death?" Leah raised an eyebrow at Raye.

"I just see death, mine and other's. It rides a vicious horse and it won't stop until we're all vanquished."

Leah stood up and put the blanket in the chair. "Okay, come on, time to go in and put on some happy music and have a shot of tequila. This shit is getting way too deep for me."

Raye finished the drink in her hand and followed Leah into her trailer. She stopped in the doorway to look up into the heavens one last time.

"I call upon the ancient powers;
To help me in this darkest hour."

Raye chanted as she entered her home and closed the door behind her.

Inside, Leah handed Raye a shot of tequila and a wedge of lime, as she held hers up for a toast. "Here's to the battle then, between good and evil, may the best bitch win!" she laughed and tossed her drink back, following it with the lime.

Raye did the same. They slammed their empty shot glasses down on the counter and the entire place shook. Leah grabbed the counter with both hands. "What in the hell is that? An earthquake?"

Jinx howled and ran into the bedroom. Raye pressed her back to the wall as the trailer shuddered and the night was filled with a deafening pounding on the metal walls and roof.

"It's not an earthquake," Raye said, looking up to the ceiling. The ground settled, the trailer was still, everything went silent. Raye slowly moved to look out the window next to the front door.

McLean stood on her patio smiling, his eyes glowing red! Raye's heart leaped into her throat. She turned to reach for her spell book, but it wasn't on the counter.

Leah stood on the other side of the room holding the spell book in her hands. "Oh, the storm's already here!" Leah said with an evil grin and a red glint in her eyes.

I hope you enjoyed the three stories of the fictional people in **FORGOTTEN LIVES**. And I hope you look forward to book two in this series: **SHATTERED SOULS:** *Where Angels and Demons Collide.*

In book two you will meet Adriana the Teacher, Chantall the Faith Seeker, and Leila the Nurturer.

Don't miss out on information for upcoming books and events by signing up on my website.

http://www.sherrybriscoe.com